"You can either come with me and listen to what I have to say or get ready to be a widow."

It took only minutes ▮▮▮▮▮▮▮▮▮▮▮▮▮▮▮▮▮ into the SUV. "Where ar▮▮▮ **W9-CBB-004**

"Someplace unusual. And public. Preferably with a crowd."

"You're scaring me, Dylan."

"Good. That makes two of us."

The Botanical Gardens, he thought. There were enough people to provide anonymity. And plenty of places to hide. Dylan sincerely hoped it wouldn't come to that.

He looked over at his wife. Watching her, he could barely breathe. Look what he'd had—and let slip away. Grace was one of a kind. Of all the mistakes he'd made, losing her had been the worst.

Grace was a sensible woman. She'd see why his future—and hers—depended on the choices he was about to make.

Now wasn't the time to reveal how much danger he was preparing to face. The less she knew about that, the safer she'd be.

* * *

WITNESS PROTECTION: Hiding in plain sight

Safe by the Marshal's Side—Shirlee McCoy, January 2014
The Baby Rescue—Margaret Daley, February 2014
Stolen Memories—Liz Johnson, March 2014
Top Secret Identity—Sharon Dunn, April 2014
Family in Hiding—Valerie Hansen, May 2014
Undercover Marriage—Terri Reed, June 2014

Books by Valerie Hansen

Love Inspired Suspense

*Her Brother's Keeper
*Out of the Depths
 Deadly Payoff
*Shadow of Turning
 Hidden in the Wall
*Nowhere to Run
*No Alibi
*My Deadly Valentine
  "Dangerous Admirer"
 Face of Danger
†Nightwatch
 The Rookie's Assignment
†Threat of Darkness
†Standing Guard
 Explosive Secrets
 Family in Hiding

Love Inspired Historical

Frontier Courtship
Wilderness Courtship
High Plains Bride
The Doctor's Newfound Family
Rescuing the Heiress

Love Inspired

*The Perfect Couple
*Second Chances
*Love One Another
*Blessings of the Heart
*Samantha's Gift
*Everlasting Love
 The Hamilton Heir
*A Treasure of the Heart
 Healing the Boss's Heart
 Cozy Christmas

*Serenity, Arkansas
†The Defenders

VALERIE HANSEN

was thirty when she awoke to the presence of the Lord in her life and turned to Jesus. In the years that followed, she worked with young children, both in church and secular environments. She also raised a family of her own and played foster mother to a wide assortment of furred and feathered critters.

Married to her high school sweetheart, she now lives in an old farmhouse she and her husband renovated with their own hands. She loves to hike the wooded hills behind the house and reflect on the marvelous turn her life has taken. Not only is she privileged to reside among the loving, accepting folks in the breathtakingly beautiful Ozark mountains of Arkansas, she also gets to share her personal faith by telling the stories of her heart for all the Love Inspired Books lines.

Life doesn't get much better than that!

Family
in Hiding

Valerie Hansen

HARLEQUIN® LOVE INSPIRED® SUSPENSE

Special thanks and acknowledgment are given to Valerie Hansen for her participation in the Witness Protection series.

Recycling programs
for this product may
not exist in your area.

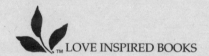

™ LOVE INSPIRED BOOKS

ISBN-13: 978-0-373-44594-3

FAMILY IN HIDING

www.Harlequin.com

Printed in U.S.A.

Suffer the little children to come unto me,
and forbid them not:
for of such is the kingdom of God.
—*Mark* 10:14

To my Joe, who will always be looking
over my shoulder as I write.
He was an extraordinary gift from God.

ONE

"Hello? Hello?"

Disgusted, Grace McIntyre slammed down the receiver. "Not funny, Dylan."

The annoying phone calls had been so prevalent lately she was thinking of changing her home number. If she hadn't figured that the harassment was coming from her soon-to-be ex-husband, she might have already done so.

She stared out the kitchen window, wistfully watching their children playing in the sunny backyard. At ten, Kyle was the eldest and had clearly been asserting more dominance over his three-year-old brother, Brandon, since Dylan had packed his personal belongings and moved out of the family home for good.

"It wasn't my fault," Grace murmured, desperately yearning to convince herself she'd had no choice but to file for divorce once she'd discovered Dylan's sinister character.

Her gaze rested on seven-year-old Beth, their middle child. The pretty little red-haired girl had grown so moody and weepy Grace was at a loss. Not that Beth was the only one shedding tears over the breakup of the McIntyre marriage. The difference was Grace had done her grieving in private, hoping to protect the children's tender emotions.

"Apparently, I haven't done a very good job," she told herself with a sigh.

The estrangement had not been sudden. She and Dylan

had been drifting apart for a long time before she'd felt the undeniable need to act. If the problem had been another woman in her husband's life, Grace believed she could have coped. But it wasn't. Dylan worshipped the god of money, of privilege, and would do anything to succeed, even if his actions meant others had to suffer—as she had sadly learned.

She dried her hands on a tea towel and turned from the window. Being personally neglected was nothing compared to facing the painful truth about her husband's underhanded business practices. His lack of remorse over what he had done had revealed Dylan's true colors and had broken her heart. The man was bright. Clever. There was no way he could have been handling the paperwork for shady adoptions and pushed through falsified documents without realizing exactly what was going on.

The aspect that had really thrown her was his easy admission of involvement. He'd acted as if he'd expected her to accept his actions as necessary and to be proud of him for bringing home hefty bonuses for bending the law. How could she have lived with that man for twelve years and have so totally misjudged him?

She blinked back tears and whirled as the back door slammed.

"Mom! Brandon's eating dirt!" Kyle shouted. "Beth told him it was a cookie."

"I did *not*." Muddy hands fisted on her hips, the little girl stomped her foot. "I was just playing house. I didn't know Brandon was going to eat anything I made."

If Grace hadn't been so downhearted to begin with, the scene of her two carrot-topped kids standing nose to freckled nose and trying to stare each other down would have made her laugh out loud. They had her stubborn streak, all right. And the twinkling blue eyes of many of their Irish ancestors. Add the McIntyre genes to that and you had a volatile genetic mixture.

Grace held up both hands. "Okay. Simmer down. Is Brandon still eating the dirt cookie?"

Beth shook her head. "No. I took it away from him." She glared at her older brother.

The smirk on Kyle's face reminded Grace of Dylan. Then again, pretty much everything did. The house they had spent a fortune remodeling was wonderful, yet not a day went by that she didn't rue her failure to ask him how they could possibly afford all the expensive improvements.

"You two go wash your hands while I get the baby and clean him up. It's almost lunchtime."

"I want peanut butter and jelly," Kyle said.

His sister made a face. "Ugh. That's all you ever eat. No wonder your face looks like a peanut."

"Does not!"

"Does so," Beth countered.

Grace clapped her hands to get their attention. "That's enough." She pointed to her elder son. "You go use the upstairs bathroom," she told him. "Beth, you use the one off the guest room. And no muddy messes, you hear? I want those sinks spotless when you're done."

Beth waited until her brother had started to turn away, then made a face and stuck out her tongue.

Grace had to smile. Kids. What would she do without them?

There had been times, particularly lately, when she'd questioned every choice she'd made since her marriage—except when it came to deciding to have children. It wouldn't be easy raising them alone. She'd have to find a job and probably sell the house. But they'd get by. Even if Dylan was out of the picture, she knew he'd still help support them. He had never been stingy.

"Unless he ends up in prison for what he did," she muttered, stepping into the yard in search of her three-year-old.

"Brandon? Where are you?"

Although he didn't answer he was easy to find by following the sound of his giggles. Standing on tiptoe, he was splashing in a concrete birdbath, clearly delighted as water flew in all directions.

"Well, at least you're cleaner than I expected," Grace said, scooping him up from behind and carrying him toward the house with the wettest, muddiest parts turned away from her green silk blouse and designer jeans.

She kicked off her sandals at the door and carried the little boy to the kitchen sink where he obligingly held his hands under running water.

His giggling was infectious. "You are one dirty kid, you know that?" she said between soft laughs.

"Kyle helped me," the child replied.

"I'm sure he did."

Grace reached for paper towels to dry off her youngest. Kyle had never been an easy child and the older he got, the more he tested her patience. He had been acting even worse since Dylan had sat everyone down and told them he was leaving. Beth had wept and Brandon had sniffled. Kyle, however, had merely stood there, jaw clenched and eyes flashing, glaring at his parents.

The boy was angry. Grace understood. She wasn't pleased with the way things had worked out, either, but there was no way she'd ever be able to forgive her husband for always putting his work before his family no matter how much they needed him at home.

Dylan had had a good job with a prestigious law firm and had been on his way up the corporate ladder, just as they'd planned, but somewhere along the way he'd lost sight of the underlying reasons for his hard work. And now? Who knew? It wasn't only that he'd destroyed his own future, he'd ruined his entire family's, too. Thrown it away as if none of them had ever mattered as much as making a lot of money.

It was always the money, first and foremost. She couldn't count the number of times she'd fed the children, then eaten a burned dinner alone because Dylan had been too involved in some hot-shot business deal to bother to come home as promised.

Truth be told, her husband had been absent so often there was little difference between their present situation and the times when he'd still lived there.

Grace sighed. That wasn't quite true. Back then, she'd always had hope he'd eventually show up. Now she knew he was gone for good. And once their divorce was final, probably the only times she'd encounter him would be when he picked up the kids on visitation days.

"Well, it is what it is," she murmured, setting her youngest at her feet and taking his hand. "Come on, honey. Let's go get you some clean clothes before lunch."

"I want a boy cheese sandwich," Brandon said, making his mother smile at the inside joke. He'd mistaken the word "grilled" for "girl" and had refused to eat the melted cheese sandwiches until Dylan had realized the problem and changed the name of the toasted treat.

"Okay," Grace said. "I'll cook you a boy cheese and Beth can have a girl cheese."

Kids. No matter how heavy life got, they were always able to lift her spirits and remind her that the most important job she had was being a mother.

The telephone began to ring again.

Grace ignored it.

Kyle rounded the corner into the kitchen and passed his mother at a run. "I'll get it. Maybe it's Dad."

"Well, if it is, tell him I'm busy."

The boy's enthusiastic expression twisted a figurative

knife in Grace's stomach as he snatched up the receiver with a breathless, "Hello? Hello, Dad?"

Grace saw Kyle's expression sober. Heard him say, "Nah. He's not here."

She paused. "Who is it?"

Kyle was hanging up. "Some guy. He said he wanted to talk to Dad."

"Well, don't worry. I'm sure he can reach him at the office if it's important."

The child's cheeks were rosy, his eyes wide. "I hope not. He sounded real mad."

"How could you tell? What did he say?"

With a quick shake of his head, Kyle answered, "No way. If I talked like that you'd wash my mouth out with soap." He eyed the phone. "That was one scary dude."

Dylan had spent the previous week in custody, being interrogated by local police as well as the U.S. marshals and FBI. By the time he'd learned enough to accept his own culpability, he'd been forced to accept the wild claims of the former missionary who had recently broken the disturbing truth to him by telephone. He was in deep trouble, legal trouble, and it looked as if there was no way out other than to confess and ask for mercy.

"Look, I've already told you," Dylan insisted, facing the authority figures who kept asking the same questions over and over. "I don't know anything about any kidnappings. I had no idea there was anything criminal about where those babies came from. For the most part, the paperwork was impeccable. I certainly had no indication a crime was involved in the cases where there were some minor omissions." He stared at the St. Louis police detectives and other nearby officers, willing them to understand the rationale behind his prior behavior.

Like it or not, the fine line between merely doing his job

versus being an upstanding citizen had blurred over time. Finding himself on the wrong side of the law had triggered an unwelcome surge of well-deserved guilt and had led Dylan to do some serious soul-searching.

"Did you tip somebody off?" one of the detectives asked.

"How could they have? You've had me isolated ever since you picked me up."

"Then why were there were no records of any of the questionable adoptions in your office files by the time we convinced someone there to look for them?"

Dylan frowned. "There weren't?"

The dark-haired young woman who had been introduced as U.S. Marshal Serena Summers shook her head. "No. None. Can you explain why that is?"

"No." Dylan was truly at a loss. "Are you sure?"

Nobody laughed at his ridiculous question, leaving him with the disappointing conclusion that someone had disposed of any incriminating evidence. That was that, except...

He cleared his throat, determined to make his interrogators take notice. "Look. It doesn't matter what happened to the originals. I have copies of everything that passed through my hands regarding those adoptions you're asking about."

"Where?"

"In my office. I can go get everything you need."

"And you expect us to let you waltz out of here, just like that?"

"If your people couldn't locate my private files, I'm the most logical one to retrieve them. Otherwise, they might disappear like you claim the other records have."

"He has a point," a detective offered. "Once we have to actually serve the subpoena, all the suspects will be alerted."

"I still don't like it." Marshal Summers shrugged beneath the padded shoulders of her tailored jacket. "However, if he's willing to sneak back in, I don't see any reason to prevent his trying to help us. We can post men in the lobby and pick him up when he comes out."

"I really do want to make amends," Dylan said with feeling. "As long as no one suspects me of working with the police, I can't see any problems, can you?"

"Actually I can see plenty," the lead detective grumbled. "But it's the Feds' call. If you want him to go, I'll agree to release him to you."

That was how Dylan ended up back at his apartment to change clothes and shave before being escorted to his office at Munders and Moore, L.L.C., via taxi.

In retrospect, he felt it was possible that at least some of the clues might lead back to Frederick Munders' wife, Matilda, who ran Perfect Family Adoption Agency. The puzzle was how an overtly open and honest woman like her could have gotten involved in baby stealing. It didn't make sense. That was a big reason why Dylan hadn't suspected the risks to his own conscience until he was in way over his head.

Thoughts of his three children brought somber reflection. How devastated those other parents must feel to have lost custody of their babies! When he'd believed that the adoptions were voluntary, he'd had no trouble bending the rules to expedite transfers of guardianship. Now, however, he knew better.

Straightening his tie and running a palm over his dark hair to make sure he was presentable, he left his plainclothes escort and entered the modern high-rise containing the law offices where he was ostensibly still employed. As long as nobody asked him what he'd been doing on his recent days off he figured he'd be okay.

He mopped his brow with a linen handkerchief before tucking it back into the breast pocket of his custom-tailored blazer, stepping onto the elevator and pressing the button for the fourth floor.

Everything seemed quite ordinary when he disembarked. The firm's prim receptionist merely nodded to him as he passed, while clerks and paper-pushers overlooked his passage the way they usually did when they were busy.

Dylan's private office was bigger than a cubicle but far smaller than that of his boss or the other senior partners. He paused in the doorway, taking care to avoid attracting undue attention, then sidled through and quietly shut the door behind him.

Nothing seemed to have been disturbed until he crossed to a filing cabinet and opened it. Everything pertaining to the adoptions the police had asked about had been removed. It hardly mattered that the files were gone, however, because it wasn't the actual paper copies the police needed, it was the private background information they contained. That, he could provide.

Going quickly to the golfing trophies atop his bookcase, Dylan unscrewed the base of one of them and withdrew a USB flash drive from a hollow space. His hands were shaking so badly he had trouble reassembling the award properly but he managed to cobble it together enough to withstand a cursory inspection.

Pocketing the drive, he wheeled and headed for the door. All he could think of was getting out of there ASAP.

He'd almost reached the elevator when he heard someone shout a gruff, "Hey!"

The doors slid open with a whoosh. Ignoring the urgent-sounding summons, Dylan stepped into the elevator and pushed the button for the lobby.

His last glimpse through the closing doors was of a uniformed security guard. The man had a hand on the butt of his holstered gun and was hurrying toward him.

It didn't matter why the guard was alerted or who might

have questioned his presence. All Dylan could think of was escaping. He punched other buttons, hoping he hadn't been too late to override his original selection.

Slowing, then coming to a smooth stop, the elevator doors opened onto the third floor. The number two was still lit on the panel, so Dylan paused rather than disembark on three. A normal person who was being chased would get off as soon as possible and take to the stairs. Logically, so would the guard who had missed the elevator. Therefore, he had to think of some other way to elude his pursuer.

By the time Dylan reached the second floor the answer had come to him. There was a back entrance to the building's barber shop with a stairway leading to and from the street. It was meant for tenants only, particularly for attorneys who wanted to avoid lurking reporters and other nuisances. This time, it would be his escape route.

He pounded down the concrete steps and burst out onto the busy sidewalk, quickly moving away. *Made it!*

When he thought about delivering the flash drive, however, he realized he had inadvertently ditched his covert police escort when he'd fled from the guard. There was no way he dared backtrack at this point. Worse, he looked every bit the professional man that he was. If someone from Munders and Moore really was after him it would be hard to hide. Not only were the police going to be looking for him soon, lots of people around there knew him on sight, too.

Reaching for his wallet, he wished the police had seen fit to return his cell phone so he could at least call for help. He ducked into a drugstore to buy sunglasses and whatever else he could find that would alter his appearance. He was paying for the glasses and waiting for the clerk to cut off the tag when he spied the answer to his unspoken prayers.

A young man wearing a tattered red St. Louis Cardinals jacket and cap stepped up behind him at the register with a bottle of soda in hand.

"A hundred bucks for the jacket," Dylan said, flashing a bill as proof and shucking his navy-blue blazer.

The youth began to grin. "Twenty more gets you my hat, too."

"Done." Dylan handed over the money as well as his own expensive coat and tie. "Here. Take these. I won't need them."

"How about my shoes?" the guy asked.

Dylan ignored him and told the salesclerk, "Keep the change," donning the silky red jacket as he raced for the door. By the time he was outside he had put on the sunglasses and pulled the bill of the cap low over his forehead.

Now what? He knew he should immediately hail a cab and return to the authorities so they wouldn't think he was trying to pull a fast one and get away from them.

Yes, he would go back. Soon. But there was something even more important to do first. He had to talk to Grace in person. To explain why he'd done what he'd done—and how he was determined to make amends. Somehow.

Granted, it probably wouldn't make any difference to her at this point, particularly because he'd have to tell her he'd been in police custody, as well. Yet he desperately wanted her to know how penitent he was and that he was already aiding the authorities as best as he could.

That kind of truth had to be conveyed face-to-face, Dylan decided. There was no way he could ever convince Grace of his change of heart over the phone. Even looking straight into her eyes was no guarantee of success. But he had to try. He simply had to. Her opinion of him mattered more than anyone else's and if he waited until after he'd turned over the flash drive he might not get that chance to speak with her privately.

Lacking an available taxi, he boarded a bus and took a seat. Just as the driver was pulling away from the curb, several more security guards burst from his office building and gathered on the sidewalk, talking into handheld radios and gesturing as if making plans for his capture. They might not know why he'd visited the office but they certainly seemed upset about it, meaning that someone must have an idea what he was after, despite not being aware of his secret files.

Dylan lowered his head to hide beneath the bill of the cap and used his hand to block the rest of his face.

His kids would be getting out of school soon and Grace would take Brandon with her to pick up Kyle and Beth. It was the only time he could be certain of catching her away from home—and away from the authorities who probably already had the family home under surveillance since he'd just given them the slip.

Gripping the back of the seat in front of him he watched the downtown pass and the suburbs begin. Almost there. Almost to his Gracie.

The thought of her pet name sobered him even further. He'd tried to be a good husband, yet his efforts had never seemed sufficient. It was just like when he was growing up. There was never enough of anything. Dylan had vowed that that would never happen to his family and it had not.

What about now? His jaw clenched. Now, his greatest desire was to stay out of jail—and to see that his loved ones were safe and well cared for. Even if his efforts to make amends were going to place him in jeopardy, he was certain his family would be safe. After all, he was no longer living at home or taking an active part in their daily lives so there was no reason for anyone to bother them, other than perhaps the police.

If he hadn't been positive that God had given up on him long ago, he might even have closed his eyes and prayed for divine help. It was hopelessness, and well-deserved guilt, that stopped him.

* * *

Grace parked in the shade across from the school and released her three-year-old from his booster seat. His pudgy little arms encircled her neck and he hugged her tightly, inadvertently pulling her long red hair as she lifted him.

"Ouch," Grace said with a smile and a toss of her head. "Easy, big boy."

"I love you, Mommy."

"I love you, too, Brandon. Just try not to pull Mama's hair, okay?"

"Okay." He leaned back and pointed. "There's Beth."

"I see her." Toting her youngest, Grace crossed to the lawn in front of the elementary school where they joined her daughter. "Have you seen Kyle?"

"Nope." Beth reached into her pink backpack and pulled out a handful of papers. "I got an A in spelling. And look what I drew."

"Very nice, honey."

"It's me and you and Daddy and the boys," the girl said proudly. "See? I gave Kyle an ugly face 'cause he's always so mean."

Grace did her best to ignore the child's telling portraits. Not only was the family still complete in her daughter's eyes, she'd noted the chip on Kyle's shoulder.

It wasn't hard to spot her eldest. His red hair stood out like a lit traffic flare at an accident scene when he left the main building and started in her direction. Then he paused, pivoted and ran right up to a total stranger.

The man crouched to embrace the boy, setting Grace's nerves on edge and causing her to react immediately. She grabbed Beth's hand and pulled her along while still balancing Brandon on one hip.

"Hey! What do you think you're doing?"

The figure stood in response to her challenge. The brim of a cap and dark glasses masked his eyes, yet there was something very familiar about the way he moved, the breadth of his shoulders, the faint shadow of stubble on his strong chin.

Grace gaped. It couldn't be. But it was.

"Dylan?"

He placed a finger against his lips. "Shush. Not here. We need to talk. Where's your car?"

"Across the street. Why? Where's yours?"

"I took a bus. It's a long story."

When he removed the glasses, Grace was startled to glimpse an unusual gleam in his eyes, as if he might be holding back tears—which, of course, was out of the question, knowing him.

"If you want to speak to me, you can do it through my lawyer the way we agreed."

Dylan replaced the glasses and spoke decisively. "This has nothing to do with our divorce. It's much more important than that."

Grace's first reaction was disappointment, followed rapidly by resentment. "What could possibly be more important than our marriage and the future of our children?" She knew her raised voice was attracting attention but she didn't care. "This is precisely why I filed for divorce, Dylan. You have always put other things ahead of your family. Why can't you see that?"

"I'm beginning to realize that my priorities need adjustment, but that's not why we have to talk. In private."

"What could you possibly have to say to me that can't be said right here?" She knew her husband well enough to tell that he was struggling with something and, in spite of her anger, she felt a twinge of pity.

"Let me put it this way, Grace," Dylan said quietly, cupping her elbow and leaning closer. "You can either come with me and listen to what I have to say or get ready to save a bunch of money because you probably won't have to pay your divorce attorney."

"Why on earth not?"

Dylan scanned the crowd and clenched his jaw before he said, "Because you'll be a widow."

TWO

It took only minutes for the McIntyre family to return to the family's midsize white SUV. Grace secured little Brandon while Dylan made sure the other two were safely belted on either side of the toddler's booster seat in the second row.

"If you want me to drive, I'll need your keys," Dylan said.

"Why? What happened to yours?"

"The same thing that happened to my briefcase and cell phone," he replied, holding out his hand.

She pulled a ring of keys from her jeans' pocket and tossed it to him. "Okay. But this better be good."

He nodded. "Get in and buckle up."

"Where are we going?"

"Someplace unusual. And public. Can you think of any nearby locations you and I have never visited?" He started the car and pulled into traffic, narrowly missing a passing motorist. "Preferably one with a crowd."

"You're scaring me, Dylan."

"Good. That makes two of us."

With an eye on his mirrors as well as the road ahead, Dylan headed west on Highway 44. "How about the botanical garden? You used to say you'd like to go there sometime and we never got around to it."

"Fine. Whatever." Grace set her jaw and folded her arms across her chest, clearly defensive. "I suppose you're going to make me wait until we get there before you explain what's going on."

He met her stare and angled his head back toward their children. "I think that's for the best. Once I've told you everything, I know you'll agree I'm doing the right thing."

"I'd better."

Continuing to cut in and out of traffic whenever it was safe to do so, Dylan remained on full alert. Not only were criminals probably after him, so was the law. He knew he shouldn't have ditched his handlers but once he'd reached the street outside his office, his heart had insisted he go straight to Grace and his children while he was still free to do so.

He caught sight of Kyle in the mirror and his gut clenched. If Grace was upset, their son was doubly angry. The boy's brow was furrowed and he was glaring at his father as if he'd already forgotten how glad he'd been to see him.

The turnoff on Shaw Boulevard took them straight to the Missouri Botanical Garden. "What section?" Dylan asked, attempting to keep the concern out of his voice. "I understand the irises are in full bloom right now."

"No," Grace replied with an audible sigh. "Make it the Children's Garden. That will give the kids something to do and we won't have to stay long. I think they close early this time of year."

"Okay. You go buy the tickets and I'll bring the kids."

Watching her shoulder her purse and slowly start toward the entrance, Dylan could barely breathe. Look what he'd had—and let slip away. Grace was one of a kind. A loving wife and a great mother. Of all the mistakes he'd made, and there were plenty, letting his work take precedence over his family had been the worst.

It was more than that, his guilty conscience insisted.

You let yourself be blinded by the promise of success and wealth beyond your dreams. And now look where you are.

Straightening with Brandon on one hip and the older children close at heel, Dylan started for the entrance to the gardens. Judging by the number of cars present they had made a good choice. There were enough others there to provide anonymity without a crowd overwhelming them. And, if necessary, the gardens would provide plenty of places to hide.

Dylan sincerely hoped it was not going to come to that. If he'd had the slightest inkling that they were being followed he would have driven straight to the nearest police station and turned himself in.

However, since they seemed to be in the clear for the present he was going to carry out his plan. Grace was a sensible woman. She'd see why his future—and hers—depended upon the choices he was about to make. Given the lives those criminals had ruined and the children they had kidnapped, according to the police, he could hardly wait to help put them all behind bars.

Finished at the ticket booth, Grace turned back to her family. Dylan saw her hair catch the rays of the afternoon sun and gleam like burnished copper, afire with highlights that gave her a haloed appearance and made him rue the poor choices that had led them to that moment.

As much as he would have liked to appeal to his alienated spouse on a personal level, he realized that this wasn't the right time to reveal how much trouble he was in and that he was preparing to face danger.

The less she knew about all that and the more he nurtured their estrangement, the safer she, and his children, would be.

Hardly anything would have surprised Grace more than her husband's presence at the elementary school. She could count on the fingers of one hand the number of times Dylan had picked up the kids. So what had brought him this time? And why was he dressed like a refugee from a Cardinals' baseball game?

She held up the brochure she'd been given with the tickets and pointed to it. "Let's go to number ten. It's an elevated pavilion. We can stand up there and watch while the kids check out the tree house and the frontier fort."

"Works for me."

Grace led the way, noting that her usually rambunctious children were clinging close to the daddy they hadn't seen in weeks. Although she felt slightly abandoned she could understand their feelings. They'd missed Dylan. So had she. Not that she'd ever actually admit it.

They started up a boarded walkway that was edged with a rough-cut rail fence and Grace wished she'd worn more substantial rubber-soled shoes rather than skimpy sandals.

She faltered once, catching herself on the bordering fencing.

"You okay?" Dylan asked.

Why did he have to be so nice? Why couldn't he be standoffish and aloof the way he used to be?

Because he's trying to drive you crazy, her imagination replied cynically. *And he's doing a wonderful job of it.*

"Grace?"

"I'm fine. Let's just get this over with, shall we?"

They reached the covered pavilion. Grace turned to her family. "Put Brandon down so he can go with Kyle and Beth."

The three-year-old clung to his daddy's neck. "No. I wanna stay here."

More tenderly than Grace had ever seen Dylan behave in the past, he set the child on his feet and kissed his damp cheek. "I'll be right here, buddy. You go with Kyle and your sister. Mommy and I need to talk."

The child clapped his hands over his ears and sniffled. "I won't listen. See?"

Kyle took him by the wrist and tugged him away, letting Beth follow at her own pace while Brandon began to whimper. Grace couldn't tell what the older boy said to quiet his brother but the whining stopped as if someone had shut off a faucet.

"All right. We're alone," Grace said. "The park closes in forty-five minutes. I'll give you thirty to tell me what's going on and then the kids and I are out of here."

Dylan shoved his hands into the pockets of the silky jacket and paced away from her before turning. "It's complicated. I hardly know where to start."

"Maybe I can make it easier for you," she said wryly. "I already know you were up to your neck in illegal adoptions because the police interviewed me about it. What more can there be?"

"Plenty," Dylan said, swallowing so hard she could see his Adam's apple move. "And it's much worse than I'd thought. Learning the truth is what finally decided it for me."

"Just wanting to be an honest, upright citizen wasn't enough for you?"

"Unfortunately, no," Dylan admitted, "although I've since had a long talk with myself and I promise I'll never step that close to the line again."

"Close? Ha! You were balancing on the sharp edge of a knife blade, Dylan. It's a wonder you didn't fall off onto the wrong side long before this."

"I know. And I'm sorry. If I had it all to do over again I hope I'd make better choices." He studied the planks at his feet. "When it all began it seemed innocent enough. My part in it was technically within the law."

"Then why are we having this talk? What's changed?"

"I have," Dylan said. He removed the dark glasses and looked straight at her.

Grace was taken aback by the pain she saw in his expression, in his eyes. If they had not had the history of the past twelve years between them, she would have believed him in a heartbeat. "Why?"

Watching his internal struggle, Grace was almost tempted to go to him and put her arms around his waist. She resisted. Waiting. Listening. Never dreaming he'd have anything earth-shattering to reveal.

When Dylan said, "Because the children involved came from a baby-stealing ring," she had to put a hand on the railing to keep her balance.

"Babies?"

It was barely spoken aloud, yet Dylan nodded. "Yes. I just found out. That's why I decided to volunteer to provide the proof the police need to put a stop to it." He paused. "I was hoping you'd be pleased."

"Flabbergasted is more like it," Grace said, glancing over his shoulder to watch her own children play. "I can't even imagine what those poor mothers went through."

"I can. I spoke with a friend of one of them on the phone. She got involved when she was a missionary in Mexico. The authorities are still trying to trace a baby she swears was taken, brought to the States and sold."

"That's terrible!"

"There's more." He reached for her hand and she let him grasp it for a few seconds before pulling away and folding her arms.

"Go on. It can't get much worse."

"Yes, it can. One of the men who had been trying to silence her—his name was Flores—was arrested and then murdered. In *jail*. So the authorities are no closer to nailing the higher-ups than they were before."

A heaviness settled in her chest. "You know who they are, don't you?"

"I have a fair idea about one or two. There's still a lot of legwork to do but I think I'm the key. So do the cops." He put his hand in his pants' pocket and pulled out the flash drive to show her. "This is why I'm not in custody today. I was picking up this evidence for them."

"Now what?" With a shiver she couldn't stop, Grace began to scan the nearby grounds as if sensing imminent threats.

"I keep a low profile and wait, I guess. Once I've turned over these files to the cops they won't need me anymore." Dylan snorted derisively. "Of course I'll have to find another job. I doubt my bosses will condone my change of heart."

"Will you be safe?"

"Don't tell me you care."

"Of course I do. The kids are already struggling to adjust because you're not in their lives. What will it do to them if you go to prison?"

"I don't expect that to happen," Dylan said. "At least I hope it won't since I have something crucial to plea bargain with."

"Does anybody else know you have evidence?"

"Not directly. I was noticed when I went by the office this morning but my regular files had been cleaned so nobody can possibly imagine what I was doing."

"You hope." Grace's emotions were on a rollercoaster and she could envision a precipice at the end where the track vanished. And Dylan with it.

She started to pace. "What am I supposed to do about the divorce if you're not around?"

"Go ahead without me," Dylan said. He shrugged so nonchalantly she wanted to scream before he added, "Of course you could postpone the final decree and see if you really need it."

"Because you expect to be murdered like that other witness who was killed in jail? Is that what you were thinking when you said I might become a widow?"

"Let's just say there's an element of risk."

His nonchalant attitude galled. "I can't believe this is happening, Dylan. If you don't care about yourself, think of your children."

"I am thinking of them. And of all those other children whose futures changed because of me." He began to pace the gazebo floor, hitting his opposite palm with his balled fist.

"What, exactly, did you do?" she asked, worried that the answer was going to hurt worse than not knowing. Merely being associated with Dylan at this point was making her feel sullied.

"The fewer details you have, the better," he said.

"Now you're sounding like the Dylan McIntyre I know," Grace countered. "Always in charge, always sure nobody else is smart enough to grasp fundamentals as cleverly as you do."

Returning to stand in front of her, toe to toe, he grasped her shoulders. The power and resolve emanating from him momentarily took her breath away. "Stop judging me by past performances and listen to me, Grace. I only came to tell you in person because I was afraid you wouldn't believe me otherwise. I'm not going to give you any more details because I don't want to put you or the kids in danger."

"How do you know it isn't already too late?" she asked, ruing the tremor in her voice and hoping she looked far more courageous than she felt.

"Because everybody knows we've been estranged for a long time and are almost divorced. And, because nobody needs to know how the authorities are finally going to be able to prove who I answered to, why I did what I did."

She twisted out of his grip. "Get real, Dylan. If these criminals are smart enough to steal babies and get away with it, what makes you think they won't suspect you of divided loyalties?"

She watched his jaw muscles working for long seconds before he spoke again. "I have no choice," he insisted. "Even if I tried to back down at this point there's no way I could go to work and behave as if nothing has changed. It was hard enough to casually walk through the office this morning." He spread his arms, palms toward her. "Look at me, Grace. Believe how sorry I am. You have to."

Before she could form a suitable answer, there was a startling noise; a distant ping that made her husband jump.

Dylan suddenly launched himself at her, carrying them both to the wooden floor and knocking the air out of Grace. "Get off me! What's the matter with you?"

"A shot! Didn't you hear it?"

"I heard something. How do you know…?"

"The kids!" he rasped into her ear. "Go get the kids out of here while I draw their fire."

Stunned, Grace nevertheless rolled onto her knees as soon as Dylan began to stand. Watching him crouch behind the railing as if those widely spaced boards would afford adequate protection from another bullet, she was astounded by the way her heart went out to him in spite of everything.

"Now," Dylan shouted over his shoulder.

He began to sprint away.

Grace scrambled in the opposite direction toward her children. Kyle had apparently noticed the furor and had gathered his siblings together inside the walls of a miniature fort. Brandon was cooperating but Beth was screeching in protest.

Grace scooped up Brandon, grabbed Beth's hand and

barely paused before heading out the opposite side of the child-size structure and ducking into thick foliage along a garden path.

Shaking so badly she could hardly stand, she hunkered down, pulling all three children close. "Shush. We're playing a game of hide-and-seek. Don't make noise or they'll find us."

Only Kyle seemed to grasp the reality behind her actions. "Where's Dad?"

"Never mind that. Just do as I say."

The slim ten-year-old started to rise. Grace grabbed a handful of his shirt and yanked him back down. "No! You have to stay with me."

"But, Dad…"

"Your father got himself into this mess and he says he can get himself out of it, so we're going to let him." She fixed her most convincing parental stare on her eldest child, thankful to see him wilt from its effects.

What she wasn't willing to admit, to Kyle or even to herself, was how worried she was for Dylan's well-being. For his future. And for the rest of the family.

Positive her brood would stay put, at least for the present, Grace reached into her shoulder bag, pulled out her cell phone and pressed 9-1-1. Somebody had to be practical and behave like a sensible adult. While Dylan was acting as if he thought he could outrun bullets, she was going to summon proper assistance.

As soon as the call was answered, Grace began with, "I'm at the botanical gardens. We think somebody is shooting at us!"

Dylan was torn. Should he circle back to rejoin his family in the hope he could protect them? Or should he stay as far away from Grace and the kids as possible? Neither choice seemed foolproof.

He'd been listening carefully and had heard no more shots. Was it possible the whole incident had been imagined? Was he so mentally unbalanced from the stress of finding out what he'd done that he was hearing things? Ducking phantom attackers? Making a mountain out of a molehill?

His jaw clenched and he shook his head. This was no trivial matter. Even if his own life wasn't currently in jeopardy, that didn't mean he and his family would remain safe in the future. Nobody who had interrogated him had mentioned the possibility of going into the Witness Protection Program but surely that was an option. It had to be, particularly since other erstwhile eyewitnesses had been assassinated while in police custody.

Now that he thought about it, perhaps he should withhold his evidence until that idea had been discussed and his wife and children had been offered sanctuary.

The distant wail of sirens told him he had not been the only garden visitor who had sensed trouble. In a way, that was comforting. At least he could be certain he hadn't imagined the attack.

Dylan stepped onto the nearest path and started to jog toward the gates, figuring to intercept the police, explain what was going on and direct them to Grace and the kids.

Rounding the final corner he spied several patrol cars entering the grounds. He raised an arm and waved to get their attention.

A crack of sound split the atmosphere.

Dylan felt as if someone had smacked his forearm with a baseball bat.

He faltered. Staggered. Grabbed his wrist with his opposite hand and yelled, "Over here!" at the top of his lungs.

When he looked down, there was blood dripping off his fingers and dotting the path at his feet.

THREE

The wail of multiple sirens settled Grace's nerves considerably. Nevertheless she waited until she spotted a man in a police uniform before she stepped out to show herself and the children.

"You the lady who called this in?" the crew-cut officer asked.

"Yes." Grace pointed at the gazebo. "We were right over there when we were shot at."

"You and these kids?" He sounded incredulous.

"No. Me and my estranged husband. He's around here somewhere."

"You sure it wasn't him who took a potshot at you?"

"It couldn't have been. We were together when it happened."

"What does your husband look like? How was he dressed?"

"He's taller than you by a couple of inches," she reported, failing to add that Dylan also looked far more masculine and mature. "He was wearing a red baseball jacket and cap."

"You'd better come with me, ma'am." Taking one last assessing look at their surroundings, he was apparently satisfied enough to holster his sidearm. "This way."

"Have you seen him? His name is Dylan McIntyre. I'm Grace."

"Yes, ma'am. I believe he's in the parking lot with some of my team."

"Is he all right?"

When she got no answer, she grabbed the officer's sleeve. "Tell me? Was he shot?"

"I really can't say."

"Can't? Or won't?"

"We're almost there, Mrs. McIntyre. He can tell you himself."

Breath whooshed out of Grace's lungs. If Dylan could talk, then he was at least alive. At that moment she wasn't sure whether she wanted to hug him for surviving or to smack him for exposing his family to such danger. Actually, doing both sounded best.

She and the slim officer cleared the exit gates together. Three patrol cars, one black van and an ambulance were parked at intervals, with the police situated closest to the gates.

Grace's rapid scan of all the vehicles led her attention to the open rear doors of the ambulance where Dylan was being treated. He had removed the silky jacket and rolled up the right sleeve of his white dress shirt. The closer she got, the better she could tell that there was blood staining the cuff.

She stopped and turned to the closest person, a young woman wearing a tailored suit and mirrored glasses. Her dark hair was pulled back severely and Grace could see part of a holster peeking out from beneath her jacket.

"Excuse me," Grace began, waiting for a smile she didn't get, then continuing despite its lack. "That's my husband over there and I don't want to scare the kids. Could you watch them for just a few minutes so I can go punch him in the nose?"

That candid comment brought a twitch of mirth to the other woman's face. "Only if you leave some of him for me and my partner." She offered her hand. "U.S. Marshal

Serena Summers. The guy over there hovering behind the paramedics is my partner, Marshal Josh McCall."

"Dylan's in a lot of trouble, isn't he?"

The marshal nodded. "How much do you know already?"

"Only that he helped arrange some adoptions that weren't strictly legal." Grace lowered her voice to speak more privately, hoping the children couldn't overhear. "He just told me some of the babies they placed were stolen. Can that be true?"

"I'm not at liberty to discuss the case. Maybe we can talk later, after Mr. McIntyre finishes giving us an official statement." She motioned to a nearby uniformed officer. "Put these kids in the van and show them all our whistles and bells. Keep them entertained and see that they stay put until I finish up out here."

Grace frowned at her. "Hold on a second. I just wanted you to watch them while I talked to my husband, not take them into custody."

"It's for their own good. You want them to be safe, don't you?"

"Of course, but…"

"Then bear with me, Mrs. McIntyre. May I call you Grace?"

"You know my first name?"

Marshal Summers nodded sagely. "Actually, I probably know more about you and your family than you do."

"Why does that not make me feel all warm and fuzzy?"

Giving a subdued chuckle, the marshal glanced at her and smiled. "I like your attitude. Reminds me of myself."

Grace mirrored the smile, partly in reply and partly because she wanted to put her children at ease. "It's okay," she told them, primarily concentrating on Kyle. "You can be in charge until I'm done checking on your father."

"Is—is he okay?"

"You can see for yourself. He's sitting right over there talking to the ambulance attendants. Now go with this policeman and be good for him, hear?"

The child's nod was reluctant, yet sufficed.

"He's a stubborn one, isn't he?" Marshal Summers asked as they walked away.

"Kyle's hardheaded, all right. Just like his daddy."

"What about you, Grace?"

"Me? Why?"

"Do you see yourself as resilient and flexible?"

"I don't know. I've never pictured myself exactly that way but I guess the description fits."

"Good."

Grace was concentrating so hard on Dylan as they approached the ambulance, she almost failed to notice that her companion and the other marshal both circled behind her as if making themselves into human shields.

Her eyes narrowed. She stared at her almost-ex-husband, willing him deliver an honest answer when she demanded, "What in the world have you gotten us into?"

Although Dylan looked pale, he managed a contrite smile. Now that the medics had removed his glasses she could see the weariness in his eyes, not to mention the odd way they glistened. "I had to do it," he said with evident remorse.

"To deserve all those big bonuses. I know. You told me about it often enough."

Dylan was shaking his head. "No, honey. I don't mean before. I mean now. I can't walk away from this. I have to work with the police to try to stop the kidnappings."

"Of course you do."

His gaze left her and settled on the marshals. "You haven't told her what's up, have you?"

"Not yet. Nothing will be settled until we get a look at the files you just gave us."

Grace clenched her fists and almost stomped a foot. "Will somebody please explain before I go ballistic?"

"It looks like I'll be going into witness protection," Dylan said. "I'm sorry. They say it can't be helped."

"But, if they have your files, why do they need you?"

"Because I can swear to their authenticity, among other things," he said. "Hopefully, I won't be gone too long."

"What about the kids? Kyle is already beside himself over the divorce. If you drop totally out of his life, I don't know how he'll handle it."

"I'll try to call him often."

Marshal Summers spoke up, shaking her head. "No, you won't. There will be no outside contact. None. That's how the program works."

Frustrated, Grace threw up her hands and made a throaty, angry sound. "Well, at least you won't be able to harass me anymore."

"What are you talking about?" Dylan looked so puzzled it gave her pause.

"The daily phone calls. I know it was you. It had to be."

"Well, it wasn't." He looked to McCall. "Did you have our phones tapped? If so, you can vouch for me."

"Sorry. Those odd, incoming calls were from a burner phone, the kind you can buy almost anywhere, use once, then throw away."

"But there were multiple calls? Grace isn't exaggerating?"

"These past few days there were," the marshal said. "The caller didn't speak until this morning when your son answered."

Dylan frowned at Grace. "What happened?"

"Kyle was embarrassed to repeat what he heard," she said. "The guy apparently cursed. A lot."

"And you didn't think to mention it to me?"

"Why should I? I thought it was either you or a friend of yours, trying to unnerve me."

Sighing, he slowly shook his head, then bowed it. "How did we get to this point, Gracie? What did I do to give you such a low opinion of me?"

"Try consorting with criminals, for starters," she snapped back. "I don't know you at all anymore. Maybe I never did. For the kids' sake I'm sorry that you have to disappear, but I can't say I'm going to miss finding out more about your misguided career choices."

A light touch on her arm from Marshal Summers diverted her attention. "Mrs. McIntyre—Grace. I'm afraid it's not that simple."

"Of course it is. The divorce will be final soon and the kids will get over missing their daddy eventually. If I had any doubts that I was doing the right thing, they vanished when I found out what Dylan has been involved in."

"I'm not talking about your divorce. I was referring to the need for you and the children to enter witness protection, too."

"Us? Why? I didn't even suspect any of this until the police interviewed me a week ago. I told them then that I wasn't involved. I've had nothing to do with Dylan for months. And before that he kept his business practices to himself. *Now,* I know why."

"Nevertheless, you met with him today and were present when he was shot. Whoever is responsible for this attack has no way of knowing you aren't culpable, too. If you're not worried about your own safety, think of your children."

Shock was too mild a word to describe Grace's feelings at that moment. This whole scenario was the stuff of nightmares. She knew what the other woman was saying, yet her mind refused to accept it. There was no way she was going to leave everything behind and just up and vanish. What about her friends? Her mother and ailing father? Her church family? The kids were relatively happy and doing well in school. Kyle played soccer after school Thursdays and Beth was just getting interested in team sports.

Squaring her shoulders, Grace faced the marshals and said, "No. I'm sorry. We won't go."

McCall spoke aside into a radio.

Several uniformed police joined them.

Grace's arm was grabbed and cold metal encircled her wrist with a click. She stared in disbelief. They were *arresting* her!

"There is one other way we can handle this," Marshal Summers said, looking pointedly at Grace after the entire group was settled inside the van. "Participation in WitSec is voluntary for adults."

Dylan knew where this conversation was going and waited for the explosion of his wife's temper. There would surely be one. When their children were involved, Grace was as protective as a mother tiger. He saw her brows arch, felt so much tension emanating from her it was almost palpable.

Her eyes narrowed. "Meaning?"

"Meaning, you can refuse to be relocated. However…"

"Why am I getting the feeling you're about to add something I'm not going to like?" Grace asked.

Serena Summers gave a slight shrug. "We do have some room to maneuver when it comes to juveniles. A judge can rule that said juveniles be made wards of the court for their own good and be forced into witness protection."

"You can't be serious. You're threatening to take my children away from me?"

"Not exactly. You're welcome to stay with them wherever they go. But rest assured, Mrs. McIntyre, they *are* going."

Observing Grace's face, Dylan saw myriad fleeting expressions come and go, ending with resolve. She raised her chin and stared at the marshals. "Then so am I."

"I'm glad you've decided to see things our way, ma'am," Marshal McCall said, sounding relieved. "It will make our task much easier."

"I'm not doing this for anybody but my children," Grace insisted. She glared over at Dylan. "Naturally, we won't be housed together, particularly once the final divorce decree comes through. And the quality of the schools will have to be at least as high as the one Kyle and Beth attend here."

"Of course."

It occurred to Dylan to wonder how many witnesses tried to dictate terms to the U.S. marshals in charge of their relocation. His guess would be very few. Nor did he think it likely that the authorities would comply with Grace's demands, particularly since she was simply collateral damage rather than an actual eyewitness to the crimes against children that they'd uncovered.

He wisely kept his opinions to himself. The time would come when Grace would have to take whatever accommodations were offered and be thankful, no matter what. It didn't take much imagination to figure that her ire would then be directed toward him.

Dylan didn't care. All he could hope for at this point was that his loved ones would remain unharmed. Enough innocent victims had already suffered for his mistakes.

He had no secret death wish, yet he'd made a solemn decision when he'd realized he'd been shot. If he had to pay with his life for his sins, then so be it. Anything, as long as his family was safe.

"I'll need to pack, of course," Grace said, organizing her thoughts and making mental lists of all the things she'd have to do before she'd be ready to leave St. Louis. "I suppose we can have the kids' school transcripts forwarded later."

Marshal McCall cleared his throat. "I'm afraid you can't go home again, Mrs. McIntyre."

"What? But I have to. There are a hundred things I need to see to—canceling the newspaper delivery, stopping the mail, calling my friends to say goodbye. Everybody at church will want to pray for us, and I'll need to touch base with my mother, too."

"I'm sorry."

Her jaw dropped. She looked into each of their faces, finally settling on Dylan's. "You knew all this, didn't you? That's why you came to see us. You wanted to fix it so we'd have to run off with you."

It made no difference that her husband was shaking his head. She didn't believe him.

"Well, it's not going to work," Grace declared. "I don't care how much trouble you're in or how many government agencies interfere in my life, I am never going to change my mind about you or about the divorce. It's too late for us, Dylan. Way, way too late."

Added to that declaration was her intense disappointment in his character. While they'd been married, she had mistakenly put her trust in him. Had accepted his excuses and explanations without question, over and over again, until she'd become numb to his lies.

Well, that kind of naïveté was in the past. She was wise to Dylan's tricks. He was never going to be able to fool her again.

Leaving her friends and former life was going to be hard, yes, but not nearly as difficult as it had been to accept the truth about the husband she had once idolized, then take the necessary steps to sever their relationship.

It had nearly killed her spirit when she'd finally given up and filed for divorce. Now, in spite of the ongoing heartache, she was glad she had done so. The more distance she could put between Dylan and their children, the less his warped sense of right and wrong would exert a negative influence upon them.

The kids had to come first. As their only respectable, upstanding parent, she owed it to them—no matter how great her personal sacrifice.

One fleeting glance at Dylan told her it was going to be *huge*.

FOUR

By the time the paramedics had finished bandaging Dylan and had given him an injection of antibiotics, his arm was truly throbbing. It had occurred to him to wonder why it hadn't hurt when he'd first felt the bullet's impact. The ambulance attendants had explained that the initial shock had temporarily deadened the area.

They fashioned a sling, passed a prescription to one of the marshals and had him sign a release before they packed up and left.

Inside the black van, plans were in the making. He sat back and listened as best he could while battling the distraction posed by his pulsing arm. He'd put on a brave front for his wife and children but was rapidly approaching the moment when he was either going to have to take a pill or lie down. Or both.

He shifted his position, hoping to find relief. Instead, a stab of intense pain made him wince. And, of all people, Grace noticed.

She stared and scowled. "I thought that was just a flesh wound."

"Still hurts," Dylan admitted. "I'm okay."

"That's not how it looks to me," Grace said, transferring her attention to Marshal Serena Summers. "Can't you give him something for it?"

"We will. As soon as he's been properly debriefed,"

Summers said. "We're taking you to a safe house until we can process your paperwork and arrange for permanent transfer. Do you have any friends or family in Texas?"

Grace shook her head. So did Dylan.

"In that case, we'll proceed as planned."

Dylan could tell by the expression on his wife's face that she was already having second thoughts. When she said, "Hold on a minute," he figured the marshals were in for a talking-to.

If she had not been cradling Brandon, Dylan knew Grace would have jumped to her feet in confrontation mode. "This safe house. If *we* go there, where will you put Dylan?"

"In the safe house," McCall answered.

"Not with us, you won't."

Dylan was afraid both marshals were going to laugh, particularly when Grace made a disgusted-looking face at him. If he hadn't been in so much pain, he would have been ready to join them.

"Mrs. McIntyre," McCall said calmly, "it's our job to protect you from criminals. We're not marriage counselors or psychologists. We will provide accommodations that will keep you and your family safe. I suggest you stop thinking of yourself and start considering your children."

The look of abject astonishment on Grace's face was a sight to behold, one Dylan knew he would not soon forget. In the following moments she went from amazement to anger, then to resignation and finally penitent surrender.

Nodding, she said, "You're right. I'm sorry. I suppose he'll behave since his arm is hurt."

The bullet wound was not the only place Dylan was hurting. He cast sad eyes on his wife and slowly shook his head, taking care to move the rest of his body as little as possible. "I have never abused or even threatened you, Grace, and I'm not about to start now, with or without a bullet hole in my arm."

"I never said you had."

"You implied it." He heaved a noisy sigh. "Look. I made some big mistakes and I'm paying for them. I don't deny that. But what I did, I did for you. For our family."

"Don't try to put the blame on me," she countered. "I never told you to lie or steal or whatever else you did."

"You were always happy when I brought home those hefty bonus checks."

"Because I didn't know what you were doing to deserve them! You…you…"

Marshal McCall stepped between them. "That's enough. Both of you. You'll have plenty of time to argue once we settle you in the safe house. Right now, we need to transfer the children and their mother to one of our cars for transport."

Dylan was about to ask about himself when Grace did it for him.

"He stays with us until we've finished asking questions and have turned his computer files over to our techs to make sure they're what he promised," McCall answered. "Then, if all goes well, he'll join you."

The expression on Grace's face was cynical when she said, "I can hardly wait."

In Dylan's mind the same sentiment lurked. Only in his case, sarcasm was not involved.

Grace had no idea where a younger marshal was taking them, nor did she ask, although Kyle did pipe up once to object to their not going home. As long as she and her poor, tired babies were safe she didn't really care. Not tonight, anyway.

Picturing tough, belligerent Kyle as a babe made her smile. He'd been such a sweetie—until his sister had come along and he'd ceased being an only child. Conversely, when

Brandon had arrived, Kyle had acted delighted to have a brother on his side against the females of the household.

That ratio was normally two to two since Dylan was so seldom in the picture. His absence was one of the things that saddened her, although, in retrospect, she was glad her estranged mate had not had as much direct influence on their children as she'd had.

If her parents had been able to cope she might have called upon her own father to step in as a surrogate, but he had developed Alzheimer's and was so far gone he didn't even recognize his wife and caregiver these days. Male relatives on Dylan's side of the family were nonexistent. His late mother had raised him by herself, meaning there had never been a father figure in his young life.

Perhaps that was the crux of his problem, Grace mused. And, if he'd chosen a role model from work, perhaps someone like his boss, Fred Munders, he'd probably been looking in the wrong place. She wasn't positive, but since Fred's wife ran an adoption agency, she wondered if good old Fred might be up to his neck in this mess.

The unmarked, black sedan approached a modest-looking, darkened house on a quiet, suburban street. The driver parked in front of the closed garage door and started to get out.

"So, this is it?" Grace spoke quietly to keep from disturbing her exhausted, dozing children.

"Yes, ma'am. Please stay in the car until I tell you it's safe to get out."

"We weren't followed, were we?"

"Only by an unmarked police car, and he turned off just before we arrived so we wouldn't draw attention."

"How long will I have to stay here?"

"Until McCall or Summers tells you to move," the driver said. "You need to trust them. They're good at what they do."

"I certainly hope so. What are my instructions? Do I just

go in the house and wait? How will I know what's going on in the outside world? And what about school for the older kids? Classes were almost over for the summer but I know they're missing final exams."

"All of that will be taken care of. Wait here," the driver told her as he got out of the car.

Grace watched as he raised the overhead door, returned and pulled the car into the garage. He then moved to a side entrance to the house, unlocked the door and, pulling his gun from a shoulder holster beneath his coat, slipped into the silent house.

Grace's fingers clenched in her lap. If this place was so safe, why did he need to inspect it with a gun in hand? What had Dylan gotten them into? The more she learned, the worse the situation became. Unfortunately, at this point, there wasn't a whole lot she could do about it, either.

The agent returned. She thought he was talking to himself until she realized he was taking a hands-free phone call as he opened her door and helped her out.

"Yes, sir," he said into the headset. "Forty-five minutes. I'll get them settled and be ready when you arrive to relieve me."

"Was that your boss?" Grace asked, more for something to chat about than out of curiosity.

The agent nodded and replied as he unbuckled Brandon and handed him to her before freeing Beth. Kyle undid his own seat belt. "Yes, ma'am. Marshal McCall will be here shortly."

And that meant...? "Him and who else?"

"Mr. McIntyre and Marshal Summers, I believe."

Grace mumbled, "Peachy," belatedly noting that Kyle had observed the telling reaction. Well, too bad. She had tried more than once to explain to the children why she'd filed for divorce and had basically failed, or so it seemed. Of the three, Kyle remained the most antagonistic, which figured, since he was the oldest. The boy was ten going on thirty, thanks to having mentally tried to assume the responsibility for the family that his father had neglected for so long.

"Kyle, honey, I'll need your help with Brandon," Grace said, hoping that assigning him a task would help her son cope. "Would you please take him to the bathroom and get him ready for bed while I look after Beth?"

"Yeah, sure. Where is it?"

"Just head down that hall and you'll find everything you need," the young marshal said, pointing. "Clothes in a lot of sizes are in the closet and bureau drawers of the first bedroom. Just grab whatever you think you'll need."

Grace had progressed as far as the kitchen. It was neat and clean, but so very tiny. There wasn't even a dishwasher! How in the world was she supposed to keep house properly in a place like this? And who was going to tend the yard for them?

"How long can we expect to be stuck here?" she asked.

The officer shrugged. "Beats me. I've seen these protection programs go on indefinitely. But you won't be staying here. This is just a halfway house. A place to stage before you disappear for good."

"That kind of thing really works? I can't imagine that a determined criminal couldn't track down just about anybody he wanted to, especially if he had enough money. What are the chances we'll be found?"

"Small, as long as you follow the rules."

Picturing Kyle in particular, she asked, "What happens if somebody cheats?"

He appeared to be weighing his answer carefully before he sobered and said, "Sometimes they die."

Getting the incriminating flash drive into the right hands had definitely been a relief to Dylan. It was going to feel even better to be reunited with his family—the sooner the better.

Recorded questioning at headquarters didn't take long and he was finally given something to help dull the pain in his arm. As he had hoped, turning over the computerized files had led the authorities to halfway trust him. Besides, considering the grilling he'd received in the past few days, there wasn't anything more to add. Evidently, law-enforcement officials had realized that and were cutting him some slack because he was hurt. Now, if he could just get Grace to do the same....

As the pain subsided and he started to relax, his eyelids grew heavy and closed. He was half-asleep, slouched in a chair and cradling his arm, when he heard his name in the background.

One eye eased open enough to peer at the marshals who had been watching him. The woman, Serena, was obviously upset and not shy about letting on.

"What do you mean it's *gone?* I gave it to you."

"I know you did. And I put it into an evidence bag and tagged it right away. You saw me."

"Then where is it?"

Dylan noticed her sidelong glance in his direction before she said, "You'll have to search him again, just in case."

"He didn't take it. He can't have. He hasn't moved a muscle since you gave him his meds."

"Just the same, it can't have gotten up and walked off."

"Around here?" McCall snorted in derision. "I'm beginning to wonder. Too many witnesses have died in custody for me to believe that all these setbacks are coincidental."

"You think there's a mole in the office?"

"Don't you?"

Dylan saw her shrug before she said, "I don't know what to think. Look what happened to my brother, Daniel."

At that, McCall stiffened and turned away from her. *Strange,* Dylan thought, peering at the others and wondering if his confusion was due to the pain meds or if the situation was so convoluted he couldn't have made sense of it if he'd had his wits about him. Either way, their personal squabble was none of his concern. He had enough problems of his own at the moment.

McCall crossed to him and stopped, his arms folded in a stern, defensive manner. "McIntyre. Stand up," he ordered. "Sorry, but I need to search you."

"I don't have that drive anymore and you know it," Dylan said, dismayed to hear his words slurring as an effect of the medication.

"Well, I know I put it on my desk and it's not there now, so you're our best guess."

"Why would I take it back? Think about that for a second." Wincing, Dylan managed to stand although he was wobbly and had to use his good arm to steady himself on a nearby file cabinet.

"Yeah, I know," McCall told him, sounding truly regretful. "This search is just so we can rule you out."

"You should ask some of the people I saw milling around in here while you were fighting with your partner."

"We weren't fighting." He started to methodically check Dylan's pockets. "Who did you see near my desk?"

"Um, can't say. Sorry." Dylan rubbed his good hand over his face, trying to clear his mind of cobwebs. "Everybody was kind of blurred, like they were in a fog."

"Did you see uniforms? Badges? Jackets with U.S. Marshal printed on the back?"

"I don't think so. Everybody wore street clothes, like you and your partner." He paused, taking a shaky breath and hoping to regain some of his equilibrium. "So, who's Daniel and what happened to him?"

The ensuing pause was so long Dylan began to wonder if the man was going to explain.

McCall cleared his throat and continued with the search. "Daniel was one of us. Marshal Summers' brother. He was killed in the line of duty. You probably read about it in the papers. The story was all over the news right after it happened."

"If my mind was working normally tonight I'd probably remember," Dylan said. "Sorry."

"Yeah, so am I." The marshal backed away. "You can sit down again. I'm done. You don't have it on you."

"That's what I told you in the first place." Sinking into the chair with an oomph, Dylan fought to catch his breath as the pain ebbed and flowed in time with his pounding pulse.

"I don't suppose you made a backup copy."

"Sure did," Dylan said, shooting a disparaging look at the marshal. "And I gave it to you."

"That's what I was afraid of," McCall conceded. "Okay, we may as well take you over to the safe house since there are no files for our techs to examine right now."

"I can't remember all the adoption cases," Dylan warned. "Don't even ask me to. That's why I kept those records."

"Understood. But whether or not we find other evidence, you'll still be needed to testify."

"You are determined to get me into more hot water, aren't you?"

"You're already in up to your neck and plenty close to a boil," the marshal gibed, helping him to his feet. "Come on. Summers and I'll take you to your family."

Dylan was medicated just enough to loosen his tongue. "I haven't got a family," he slurred. "I lost 'em. Lost 'em all, just like that." A feeble attempt to snap his fingers failed and he staggered, nearly falling until the marshal righted him.

"Easy, man. I know how you feel but it won't do any good to lose sleep over it. Some things are beyond fixing."

"You sound like you know all about that."

McCall nodded as Summers joined them. Dylan saw him look straight at her as he quietly said, "Yeah, I do."

FIVE

If Grace could have slept she would gladly have done so. Unfortunately every time she tried to relax and close her eyes, she pictured her estranged husband, hurt and bleeding. That image did strange things to her stomach and actually made her a little queasy, much to her dismay.

Truth to tell, she still had a soft spot in her heart for that man. *Correction. For the man Dylan had once been.*

Those early years of their marriage had been the sweetest of her life. They had struggled together to get him through school and into a prestigious law firm that would jump-start his career. And they had succeeded, or so Grace had thought at the time. Now, it was beginning to look as if Dylan had dived into a tank of hungry sharks.

Grace still believed that upholding the law while striving for justice was a noble profession. The problem was that she could see now that Dylan had subverted it by bending the rules and had received hefty bonuses for doing so.

Perhaps, if he had merely acted out of a skewed sense of right and wrong, she'd find it easier to forgive him. Believing that his actions were predicated on financial reward rather than a desire to do the right thing pained her. There was no way she could allow her impressionable children to continue to be influenced by their father's poor choices. If she had not already filed for divorce for far less drastic reasons, it would have undoubtedly come to that in the long run, anyway.

Muted voices reached her through the half-open bedroom door in the safe house. She had chosen to remain dressed and stay with her children, and was therefore occupying a rocking chair while the boys shared one twin bed and Beth slept in the other.

Her senses heightened. She listened for a few more moments before getting to her feet and tiptoeing to the door. It sounded as if the marshals might be discussing her situation. She had to know for sure.

Slipping into the hallway, she eased the bedroom door almost closed behind her and went to join the other adults. It wasn't a surprise to see Dylan but his ashen appearance did startle her. So did the fact that he seemed only partially conscious.

"What did you do to him?" Grace demanded, approaching cautiously.

"Gave him a pain pill," Marshal Summers replied. "He needed it."

"He looks awful." In spite of herself, Grace sidled up to her estranged mate and put one hand on his uninjured shoulder while she laid the other against his forehead. "Whoa! He's burning up. You need to take him to a doctor."

Before she could remove her hands she heard Dylan sigh with contentment and felt him relax beneath her touch.

"That's my Gracie," he slurred, alternately smiling and grimacing. "Always taking good care of me."

She forced herself to ignore him and concentrate on the marshals. "I'm serious. He's running a fever. Just look at him. You can see he's sick."

"The paramedics gave him an antibiotic shot when they treated him. He'll be fine," McCall said. Both marshals nodded.

Their attitude angered her. "I know you already got what you wanted from him but that's no reason to let him suffer."

It was the regretful expression on Marshal McCall's face that led her to ask, "You did, didn't you? I mean, I saw him hand you the flash drive with the files on it. What more can you want from him?"

"Lost it," Dylan murmured, adding a chuckle. "They up and lost it."

Grace was flabbergasted. *"What?"*

"Never mind. That's our problem, not yours." Serena Summers slipped into the open area that served as kitchen and dining nook. "Anybody hungry?" She opened the refrigerator and leaned to peer into it. "Looks like sandwiches are our only choice but the fixings are still in date. That's a plus."

Grace stood her ground. "I don't believe you people. How can you eat when there are criminals out there just waiting for us to make a mistake? Look what they did to Dylan!"

She was aware that she still had one hand resting on his shoulder but decided to keep it there, as if her touch might somehow have a therapeutic effect. She might be so disappointed in him that she could scream, but that didn't mean she was going to stand by and let him be mistreated.

"We all need to eat," the female marshal said flatly. "Nobody is at his or her best when they're hungry and tired. The hungry part I'm about to take care of. Sleep will be up to you, Mrs. McIntyre. I suggest you get as much rest as possible while Josh and I are still with you. Once you complete your permanent relocation we won't be there to hold your hand."

"I don't want my hand held," Grace said, unable to keep the rancor out of her tone. "I want my life back."

The resolute looks both marshals gave her spoke volumes. They might as well have come right out and said,

"That is never going to happen," because that was what Grace was finally starting to realize. It was all over. She and her children were never going to be the same, never going to share that wonderful big house that she and Dylan had labored so hard to remodel, never going to feel totally well, totally secure again.

And it was all his fault.

Pensive, Grace reminded herself that her Christian faith required forgiveness. Perhaps, in the long run, she could have forgiven Dylan for neglecting his family and even for acting foolishly in regard to some adoptions. But he had also aided and abetted baby stealing and his criminal actions had cost his family literally everything.

That, she could never, ever forgive.

Dylan spent the night napping in a reclining chair because the more upright position eased the pain in his wounded arm. By morning he was feeling much better—as long as he didn't forget and move too rapidly.

The aroma of freshly brewed coffee brought him out of a fitful sleep. He opened his eyes and spotted Grace in the kitchen. Her back was to him.

The urge to stretch was strong in spite of knowing it would hurt to do so. Dylan raised his good arm and yawned. "Morning."

Grace spun, her eyes wide. "You scared me."

"Sorry. Why are you cooking? What happened to our babysitters?"

"They left early. There's an unmarked police car parked down the street, just in case."

He had to smile in spite of himself. "You let them go and leave us here together? I'm surprised."

"Not as surprised as I was when they said goodbye," Grace countered, scowling at him.

"So, what's plan A?"

She picked up a blue prescription bottle and held it out to him. "You're supposed to take one of these pain pills every four hours, with food, which is why I'm making breakfast."

"Thanks."

"Don't thank me. And don't get any ideas, Dylan. This is only a temporary arrangement. They're supposed to be back this afternoon with our new identities and instructions."

Sobering, he drew a glass of tap water and downed one of the capsules before choosing a slice of buttered toast and taking a bite. "If my arm wasn't in a sling I'd put jam on this."

Grace's movements were jerky when she grabbed the toast from him and hurriedly slathered it with blackberry preserves. "There. Anything else?"

He knew better than to bother telling her he had merely been making polite conversation, not asking her to wait on him. When Grace was in a snit like this, she wasn't the most rational person in the world.

Then again, he mused, she had good reasons for being out of sorts. If he had been able to go back in time and erase his errors, he would have. But there was no way to do that. And no way to get Grace and the kids out of the mess he'd created by making the wrong choices.

The worst part of this whole situation was that he'd known he was taking a chance by accepting paperwork that he'd not been totally comfortable with, yet he'd proceeded. Signed off on it. Sent it on to a judge who had then approved the shady adoptions.

Judge Simon Simms had handled most of those cases so he was probably going to be in hot water, too, although, like Fred Munders, the judge could always claim he'd trusted the information on the forms that had been submitted to him. Which pointed the finger of guilt right back at Dylan McIntyre.

"Looks like I was set up," he muttered to himself. "And I walked right into the trap."

"What did you say?" Grace asked.

Dylan shook his head and took a sip from the coffee mug she'd filled for him. "Doesn't matter. I was just thinking out loud."

"You sound a lot more lucid this morning," she commented. "How's the arm?"

"Tolerable. I'd like to cut back on my pain medication if I can, just in case I need my wits about me."

He saw her shiver. "Do you really think someone is trying to kill you?"

Glancing at the bandage on his arm, he arched his eyebrows. "What does it look like to you?"

She pressed her lips into a thin line an instant before she turned away muttering.

"What? I didn't hear that."

"I said, it looks like your bad choices are coming back to haunt you, Dylan. I just wish I'd had the courage to leave you years ago."

"You can't mean that. We had some really good times, didn't we?"

"I had a lot of dreams that you made come true," she admitted, glancing at the hallway leading to the bedroom where their children slept. "But they sure didn't include going on the run to escape murderers and kidnappers."

"I said I was sorry. If there was anything else I could do to fix things, you know I would. I love…I love the kids, too."

And he still loved Grace, in spite of their estrangement. Yes, most of their problems were of his making. And, yes, he had neglected his family in favor of hard work at Munders and Moore, but that made him a workaholic, not a criminal. It wasn't a lack of morals that had pushed him to accept records that he should have suspected as being bogus, it was his desire to please his boss and the firm's clients.

In retrospect, Dylan could see lots of red flags that should have alerted him to the true facts. One, there was a sudden influx of available young children and babies, which had been fairly scarce before. And, two, there was an uncanny similarity in their original home situations. The ease with which their reported birth mothers had given them up was highly unusual. Either those women had been coerced somehow, or worse, they were phantom surrogates who didn't actually exist.

He moved his injured arm and winced. *I deserve everything I get,* he mused, disheartened, realizing that Grace was absolutely correct. He and he alone had brought this catastrophe down on his loved ones.

And he alone would have to stand up to organized crime and testify, even if it cost him his life, to ultimately save everyone else he cared about.

He only hoped that God would honor Grace's faith and spare her and their innocent children.

The marshals had briefed him enough to let him know there was no guarantee that the Witness Protection Program would work. They would try to safeguard everyone, of course. And he would do all he could to impress upon his family that keeping the strict rules was critical to their survival.

Beyond that, the future was out of his hands.

Dylan sighed and glanced at his wife as she stood at the stove, flipping pancakes. "Gracie?"

Her shoulders stiffened visibly before she whirled. "Don't call me that."

"All right. Grace, then. I was just wondering if you'd prayed about all this."

"What kind of question is that? Of course, I have."

"Good," he replied with an audible sigh, "because I'm pretty sure there's no way God's going to listen to me."

About to turn away and go freshen up, Dylan spied a movement through the kitchen window behind his wife. "Grace!"

"What?" Her gaze followed his. "What did you see?"

"I'm not sure. Get away from that window."

"You're scaring me."

Dylan was adamant, his heart pounding so hard he could hear the pulse in his ears. He yanked the cord and managed to lower the blinds one-handed. "How did that get pulled up, anyway?"

"I raised it. I like to see the sun in the morning."

"I'm going to call the marshal's number and report that we saw something suspicious," he told her. "You go make sure the kids are okay."

"Is this what it's going to be like for us from now on?" she rasped. "Are we always going to be dodging shadows?"

"I don't know," Dylan said, cradling his sore arm after moving it too much. "Just remember, some of those so-called shadows may be armed and dangerous."

"I hate this," she huffed over her shoulder as she headed for the hall. "And I hate you, too."

Dylan didn't bother to argue. At the moment he tended to agree with her. On both counts.

For Grace, the rest of the morning crept by like a lazy snail on tranquilizers. The police had found nothing amiss in the yard and had regarded her and Dylan with skepticism, acting as if they had purposely made a false report.

She'd dressed and fed her brood, including their father, then had cleaned up the kitchen by herself. There was no way an injured man could have assisted, anyway, and as far as she was concerned, the less she had to interact with Dylan the better she liked it.

The children were watching cartoons on a small console television in the master bedroom when the marshals returned bearing a briefcase filled with important-looking papers.

"The kids are in the back, watching TV," Grace explained. "Should I go get them?"

"Not yet." Marshal Summers laid her black leather case on the small kitchen table and clicked the locks open with her thumbs. "We'll be leaving this background info with you to memorize. You'd be smart to give it your full attention. The better you remember your new identities and the history we've prepared for you, the less chance of a slipup."

"That's going to be really hard for the kids," Grace commented. "Can they at least keep their first names?"

"If you want them to. You and Dylan should go with a full change, though. We're going to call you John and Mary…"

"Smith?" Dylan gibed. "Talk about generic."

"No, we decided on Appleby, mainly to make it easy for the older children to remember and spell."

Grace spoke up. "I hope you were kidding about John and Mary."

"Not at all. Why?"

"Because I'm named after my paternal grandmother. I intend to keep calling myself Grace, whether you approve or not."

"Then we'll make Grace your official middle name on your new social security card and you can use Mary for anything requiring a legal signature. Will that do?"

"I suppose it'll have to." She pulled a face and shot a look at her husband. "Make his name *Mud,* will you?"

That brought a wry smile to the marshal's face. "How about John D.—for Dylan—and you can call each other whatever you like in private?"

Dylan chuckled. "I don't think giving her that much leeway about what to call me to my face is a good suggestion, considering her current low opinion of me."

"Work it out," Marshal McCall interjected soberly. "You're going to have to rely on each other's discretion if you intend to survive. We're going over surveillance recordings at our office to see if anyone who didn't belong there might have been nosing around my desk when the flash drive you gave us went missing. We may be able to slack up a bit if and when we ID them, but don't hold your breath, okay?"

Nodding, Grace leaned over to scan the documents the female marshal was spreading out on the table. "Except for where we originally came from, this looks pretty easy to learn." She began to frown. "Hold it. This says we're husband and wife."

"You are," Summers reminded her.

"Not for long."

"Well, at the moment you still are, so live with it. Or maybe die by pulling out of the program, Mrs. Appleby. It's up to you, remember?"

"There *is* no choice for me if it means giving up my children," Grace countered. "I'll never do that."

When Dylan smiled slightly and said, "Good," she didn't know whether to be happy or furious with him. While she struggled and struggled to merely think straight, he seemed to be taking everything in stride, as if the whole miserable affair was an adventure.

Remembering how frightened she'd been when she'd seen him sitting at the back of the ambulance, bleeding, she shivered and felt her stomach lurch.

This was no adventure. It was a waking nightmare. One that could turn fatal at any moment.

Dylan had the bullet hole in his arm to prove it.

SIX

One of the deputy marshals had showed up at the safe house bearing brand-new carry-ons for the adults and crammed backpacks for each of the children, as well as the promised social security cards. Beth and Brandon had acted delighted about their new packs while Kyle told everyone who would listen that his was "lame."

"You'd better be grateful for anything you get," Dylan warned his eldest. "We're in the Witness Protection Program now, and, like your mother and I told you this morning, we have to play by their rules. Understand?"

The ten-year-old hung his head and mumbled, "Yeah."

"You, too, Beth, Brandon," Dylan added, using a softer tone. "Even though none of us like the idea of moving, we have to do it so we'll all be safe."

Kyle chose that moment to express himself. "So you'd better behave or they'll shoot you like they shot Daddy."

"Kyle!" Grace was adamant. "Stop scaring your sister and brother."

"Well, it's true." Kyle faced his parents with his hands fisted at his sides, as if ready to do battle for his opinion, right or wrong.

Grace sighed, then bent, opened her arms and pulled all three children closer. "This won't be forever. I promise. We just need to follow orders until the police tell us it's okay.

You've seen TV shows that explain what we're doing. The good guys will keep us safe from the bad guys."

"Even Daddy?" the youngest asked.

Dylan's breath caught for an instant when he heard his wife say, "Yes. Even Daddy."

Grace had accepted her bag graciously, checked its contents for necessities on the way to the airport and had requested nothing more. Dylan hadn't even bothered to look in his, deciding to make do with whatever was provided. At this point, he figured he was fortunate to be alive and that sobering fact minimized any other concerns.

Seated on the aisle of the aircraft with Kyle next to him and Grace and the other two children in front by one row, Dylan patted his son's knee. "At least you're getting to ride in a plane, huh?"

The boy rolled his eyes at his dad.

"If I could, I'd still go alone," Dylan said quietly. "The last thing I intended was to put you kids and your mother in danger. You know that, right?"

"Yeah, sure, Dad." Kyle turned his face to the window, effectively ending their brief conversation on a clearly cynical note.

Dylan knew he'd messed up big time without having to experience his son's rejection. Everything he'd touched lately had gone to pieces, beginning with his personal life and including his career.

As things stood, he doubted he'd ever be able to practice law again. That occupation made him far too visible, too public. Which meant that his entire education had been wasted.

Wrong, he countered. *I threw it away.*

Such a stark truth was not easy to accept, but accept it he did. Somewhere along the line he'd stepped off the right path—the "narrow way" the Bible called it—and had strayed into the dark place where he was now trapped. Where they were all trapped.

He closed his eyes to shut out reality and soon found himself pondering God's grace and His divine forgiveness. True, a man couldn't undo his mistakes, but maybe, just maybe, he could find a little peace if he repented and prayed for a fresh start.

Words failed Dylan so he let his heart do the pleading. If being so remorseful he could hardly breathe, hardly think, counted with his heavenly Father, then he was more than ready to be forgiven, to turn back to the Lord.

Questions in the remote recesses of his mind kept needling him, insisting that he was too far gone, had sinned too gravely to ever return to God's family. Yet, within him, there grew an assurance that slowly morphed into calm and brought a deep, soothing peace that seemed to flow over and through him, from the top of his head to his toes.

Dylan inhaled sharply. This must be "the peace that passes all understanding," he concluded. It was amazing. Indescribable.

Unshed tears filled his closed eyes and dampened his lashes. He dared not open his eyes for fear he might be dreaming. For fear this incredible rightness of being would vanish.

He felt a light tap on the back of the hand on his uninjured side. "Dad?"

Kyle?

Dylan slowly responded, blinking rapidly and hoping he didn't have to wipe away shed tears in front of his eldest son. "What is it?"

The boy was visibly moved. His lower lip was quivering. His blue eyes glistened. "I'm…I'm sorry, Dad. I'm not mad at you. Honest. I love you."

"I love you, too, son," Dylan whispered.

If there had been the faintest shadow of lingering doubt

that God had forgiven him completely, this unexpected conversation had wiped it away. The Lord was using Kyle to convey not only his own childish love, but divine love, as well.

It was going to be nearly impossible to explain this marvelous experience to anyone else. Dylan hardly understood it himself, other than to know without hesitation that he had taken the first step back to redemption. Maybe even back toward the happiness he'd once enjoyed and had foolishly thrown away.

That would have to suffice for the present. He let his gaze rest on what he could see of the reddish halo of Grace's hair over the seat back and felt his pulse jump. From here on he'd stop wishing away his errors in judgment and would face them squarely, knowing that God was with him again. Perhaps He always had been, even when Dylan had been too caught up in making money to heed the Lord's warnings.

"Help me find a way for the police to rescue those kidnapped children," he whispered to himself. No other elements of his legal actions hurt him as much as knowing there were mothers somewhere, perhaps women just like his Gracie, mourning their lost babies.

He now knew he had been involved in worsening their grief. He would gladly testify against anyone else who had participated, even if he had to remain in hiding for the rest of his life.

Even if doing so shortened his days on this earth.

There was no respite for Grace as the airliner sped toward Houston. Her active brain would not permit her to rest, even for a few seconds. She kept thinking of all the people she'd never see again, all the friends who would probably think the worst of her once they heard what Dylan had done and realized she, too, had disappeared.

Her own mother was going to be given a brief summary of events and told she had arranged ongoing professional care for her mentally failing father. That was the best deal she'd been able to negotiate, and, to her surprise, Dylan had readily agreed to earmark much of the proceeds from the sale of their enormous house for that purpose.

Chagrined, Grace realized that the woman she had once been was no more. The life she had led was in the past, never to return. And the future?

That was the scariest part of all this. The not knowing, not being able to plan sensibly or even to guess what to expect. She and her family were at the mercy of a government entity whose purpose was to keep them alive so Dylan could testify. Period. The officers' motives might appear fine and noble, but the underlying reason they took such pains to care for everyone had to be because it was their assignment.

So what's mine? Grace asked herself for the millionth time.

To survive. To be a mother to your children and do all you can to shepherd them through this crisis.

That was a given. And to succeed, she'd have to bend her will to that of her official guardians whether she liked it or not. She could do that much. For the kids. And because she needed to survive to look after them.

What about Dylan? her conscience prodded.

That was a very good question; one she was loath to answer. The man was like a chameleon, never showing his true colors, never being himself unless it suited his purposes. She could not trust him now. Perhaps she never could.

Hardening her heart and firming up her resolve, she vowed to remain on guard against his wiles—or those of any others. While she was caught up in this conflict she must always remain on guard. She must always be cautious about trusting anyone, even those in authority.

The marshals had claimed the files Dylan had given them had been stolen. That seemed awfully farfetched to Grace. If they couldn't trust their own people, what chance did protected witnesses have?

Like the men who had been killed while in jail, she added, thinking once again of Dylan.

Someone had already tried to kill him to silence him. In her heart of hearts, she knew they would most certainly try again.

It didn't matter how disappointed she was in him. If they succeeded in ending his life, she would weep bitter tears.

Dylan had flown into Houston's George Bush Intercontinental Airport before and knew how enormous it was. Consequently he was not surprised when their flight landed at the former Ellington Air Force Base field instead, since it was one of the two smaller choices in that part of Texas.

A flight attendant was already in position at the door when the pilot announced their arrival.

Dylan had removed his seat belt and was about to stand when he felt a firm touch on his shoulder.

"You wait here while they empty the plane," a stranger behind him ordered.

Startled, Dylan's initial reaction was to tense and prepare to do battle, until he reasoned that the marshal's office must have put someone on the plane to watch over them. That made perfect sense.

He noticed Grace stirring, so he leaned forward. "Not yet, honey. We're supposed to wait."

She was scowling when she shifted and turned to kneel on her seat to face him. "Who says? I don't remember anybody telling us that when we boarded."

"The guy behind me. In the next row." He signaled subtly with a tilt of his head instead of pointing and attracting undue attention.

"Him? You must be joking."

"Just be patient and don't get hostile," Dylan urged.

As he spoke to calm her, he also slewed in the narrow seat and glanced over his shoulder. Grace had a point. The stranger seated behind them was anything but polished and official-looking. Instead he was scruffy with a couple days' growth of beard, dark hair and eyes, and casual clothes that could have used pressing, not to mention replacing.

The fight-or-flight reaction returned in force. As soon as the aisle was clear Dylan stood and confronted the man, fists balled, muscles taut. "All right. Either show us some ID or I'll call the flight attendants and tell them I heard you plotting an attack on this plane."

Smiling, the lanky young man rose and reached into a jacket pocket for his badge wallet. "Marshal Burke Trier, at your service, folks."

Dylan relaxed when he saw it. "Okay. Sorry. You just don't look the way I'd expected."

"I can have that effect on people when I work at it," Trier said. He gestured to the empty aisle. "Now, shall we go? I'd like to get you settled and get back to St. Louis by tonight. The Cards are playing a home game and I have tickets."

Life goes on, Dylan thought sadly, *for everybody but me and my family.*

He sighed and opened the overhead bins to hand down the bags and backpacks. Sometimes he felt as if he were acting a part in a movie, simply following a script instead of participating in life. Parts of his brain felt numb. Disconnected from reality.

That was his problem, he realized. He might be up to his neck in alligators but his mind was still refusing to acknowledge that he was anywhere near a swamp, let alone about to be pulled under water for the last time and drowned by hungry gators.

He forced himself to concentrate on the present, to take it moment by moment. That was the only way he was going to make it through this, he reasoned, the only way he was going to be able to adequately defend his family if it came to that.

Dylan's heart felt as though it was being clenched by a mighty fist as he gazed at his wife and children. He'd had everything that really mattered all along and had been too blind to see it.

Pretending they were still a viable family group was foolish, he knew, yet he planned to put the time when they were forced to be together to good use. The marshals' insistence that they live as husband and wife while still technically married had made his heart sing.

At this point, Dylan didn't care what size house they ended up with or what it looked like. This was his chance to try to repair the hearts and minds he'd wounded. He would not waste this second chance.

Would Grace mourn if he lost his life? he wondered.

That thought led him straight to the other far worse possibility; the threat that had landed them where they were at present.

If anything bad happened to his family, Dylan knew his own heart wouldn't want to keep beating. He wasn't being morbid. He was simply being brutally honest.

The black SUV that transported Grace and the others through Houston to the suburbs was comfortable enough. It was the reason for the trip that was unnerving her. Everything was strange. New. Unknown. Houston was clearly a major city—not that St. Louis wasn't—yet she wondered if she was going to feel half as at home here as she had there.

"We're taking you to a neighborhood called Larchmont,"

Marshal Trier said. "It's close to shopping and schools without being too crowded. Most of the older homes that were built there in the fifties have been replaced by newer, two-story houses."

"That doesn't sound so bad," Grace replied. Judging by the dwellings they were passing, the area was fairly upscale and definitely acceptable. Landscaping was fashionable and well-tended, and the homes were quite lovely.

"I said most, not all," he told her with a chuckle. "Yours could use a little sprucing up. Feel free to do whatever grabs you. Even if you end up moving again, you'll want to make the place feel homey while you're there."

"What I'd like to do is go back where we came from," she answered wryly. The SUV was slowing and turning onto a narrow, concrete driveway. Grace took one look at the house she was supposed to move in to and gasped. "Surely not *here*."

"It'll grow on you," the marshal told them, sounding so cheerful Grace wanted to scream. "You insisted on separate quarters and this duplex was all we had available that met your demands. It's fully furnished including linen and kitchen stuff. The backyard is fenced for safety and there's a door between the two units so you can send the kids back and forth without stepping outside."

"I'm not sending my children anywhere."

"Suit yourself." He stepped out of the SUV and circled to retrieve their bags for them. "Everybody out. You're home."

Without comment, Dylan hoisted both carry-ons and started to herd the kids toward the porch while Grace remained rooted to the ground. The house's paint was flaking, the porch sagged and there were enough shingles missing from the peaked roof she wondered if it was still waterproof.

The boys and their father were approaching the place eagerly. Beth, however, clung to Grace. That was what fi-

nally convinced her to pretend she accepted the accommodations, such as they were.

She took her daughter by the hand and stepped forward,
acting as though this was not another chapter of her ongoing nightmare. The property located to one side of their
new home seemed nice enough. The house on the other
side, however, left almost as much to be desired as the duplex did.

"Who lives next to us?" Grace asked with trepidation.
Since they were being relocated, was it possible they'd been
put in a conclave of reformed crooks and other unsavory
individuals?

"Beats me. I don't do the vetting, but somebody has."
Trier handed a ring of keys to Dylan and shook his hand.
"You'll be hearing from us when we need you. In the meantime, the best thing you can do is behave as if you're exactly who we've told you to be. The more successfully you
convince the locals, the less likely they'll wonder about you
and the less chance anybody will give you away, acciden-
tally or otherwise. Is that clear?"

Grace nodded, noting that her soon-to-be-ex was doing
the same. "Are both sides of this house the same?" she
asked.

"They're close." Trier gestured. "One of the bedrooms
over here has been made into a den so you'll probably want
the other side for whoever keeps the kids." He pointed to a
small table in the entryway. "The rest of the info is in that
file over there. Mr. Appleby already has a job in a big warehouse store this side of the Galleria in the Uptown District.
We drove past it on our way here."

"What about me? I need to be home to watch Brandon, and with summer coming the other kids will be out
of school, too."

"We thought of that, Mary Grace," the marshal said with
a grin. "You were a stay-at-home mom before and that's

what you'll be now. Believe me, it's a lot safer than trying to find adequate daycare. I know. My sister went through a dozen places before she found a good one."

Frowning, Grace looked toward her husband. "Dylan has to work? At a blue-collar job? That hardly seems fair. I thought you'd be taking care of us?"

Dylan raised a hand. "They are. If I stayed home with you all the time, how would I explain my idleness? Besides, it might be a nice change of pace to ditch the starched collars and neckties. Half the time they made me feel as if I was being strangled."

What her contrary side wanted her to do was to tell him she'd like to *help* strangle him. Instead she merely nodded in apparent capitulation.

Burke Trier was already heading for the front door. "We're relying on you folks to keep your eyes open and report anything that seems out of the ordinary. Phone numbers you may need are in the file, too. Other than that, just sit tight."

Staring after him as he left, Grace realized belatedly that her jaw had dropped, so she snapped her mouth closed. "Well, I guess that's that."

"Why don't you and the kids go inspect this place and choose where you want to sleep?" Dylan asked.

She faced him, chin raised, hand extended. "First, give me the keys so I can be sure the locks work."

"You won't have to lock me out of your quarters, Grace. I won't bother you. I promise."

Her stance didn't waver.

Dylan laid the entire ring of keys in her palm and sighed. "Keep whatever you want and give the rest back to me. I trust you, Gracie."

"Mary Grace," she countered, whirling and starting for the connecting door. "Mary Grace Appleby, thanks to you."

He didn't blame her for being cross. If he'd been in her

shoes he figured he'd have lost his cool long ago. Still, they'd have to work together if they hoped to carry off this charade.

Pacing across the threadbare, living-room rug, Dylan paused at a window and lifted one edge of the heavy drapes so he could check the street. Everything seemed quiet. A couple of children were passing on bicycles and the man across the street was mowing his lawn.

Was that normal? He had no idea, which meant they could be in terrible danger and not even suspect it until it was too late.

While his family was exploring the house, Dylan decided to step outside and introduce himself to as many of his neighbors as possible. With no friends and no way to assess their tenuous situation, they were like sitting ducks. Having a few friends would be an asset.

The realization that a rifleman could be lining him up in his sights at that very moment shook Dylan to the core, made his pulse jump, brought perspiration to his brow.

Nevertheless, he stepped out onto the weathered porch and started across the street toward the lawn-mowing figure.

Hair on the back of his neck prickled. He shoved his hands into the pockets of his jeans to hide the slight tremor he couldn't totally control. When he had to wait for traffic to pass he almost changed his mind and went back into the house.

The neighbor who had been working in his yard paused, wiped his brow with his sleeve, then looked over and waved.

Now Dylan was committed. He had to proceed or attract the wrong kind of attention.

Squaring his shoulders and forcing a smile, he looked both ways and stepped off the curb.

He'd nearly reached the opposite side of the street when a

speeding motorcyclist roared around the corner on a heavy bike, headed his way.

Since he was already well in the clear, Dylan didn't pay much attention to the cycle—until its rider jerked the wheel and swerved toward him at the last minute before gunning the motor and roaring away.

Dylan leaped aside, jumping between two parked cars and landing on the newly cut grass lining both sides of the concrete walkway.

He heard his neighbor shout and curse at the rider.

Rising above that din was a clear, high-pitched shriek he recognized immediately. Grace had seen the whole thing!

Worse, she'd left the children in the house and was rushing to his aid. If this had been a trap or even a mere diversion, she had just made a critical error. One he was going to have to mention in the strongest terms once he had her alone.

In the meantime Dylan decided, getting to his feet and dusting himself off, they were about to meet their first neighbor. He hoped he'd be able to think up a valid excuse to cut the meeting short because all he wanted to do at that point was to gather up his semihysterical wife and hustle her back to their children, ASAP.

SEVEN

"Don't yell at me," Grace told Dylan once they were back in their new home. "You're scaring the kids."

"They'd be a lot more than scared if some stranger had waltzed in here and hurt them while you were busy playing Florence Nightingale across the street."

"I thought you'd been hit, okay?"

"Don't tell me you cared."

She pulled a face and planted her balled fists on her hips. There was no way she was going to admit how frightened she'd been for him when she'd seen him go down. For all she'd known, he might have been badly injured.

Instead of admitting concern and weakening her uncompromising stance, she said, "If the bad guys find you, they find all of us. Why shouldn't I be worried when something odd happens?"

"I suppose there is a certain logic to that train of thought," Dylan admitted, although Grace could tell he wasn't fully convinced.

"Of course there is. Give me some credit. You know I'm not the kind of person who acts silly and helpless the way a lot of women do."

"You're right."

Grace's eyebrows arched. "Excuse me? Did you just agree with me?"

"Yes. What's wrong with that?"

"Nothing. It took me by surprise, is all."

"Actually, I was amazed that you managed to pull yourself together fast enough to carry on a semiliterate conversation with the guy across the street."

"*Semi*literate? Please, don't overdo the compliments. Too much approval is liable to go to my head."

"I didn't mean that the way it came out," he said, seeming genuinely contrite.

"Good." Dylan looked so uncomfortable she couldn't help laughing. "For a guy who's supposed to be a whiz at courtroom debate, you sure seem to be having trouble expressing yourself lately."

"That's because I can detach my mind from my feelings when I'm working," he explained. "But when it comes to you and the kids, it's different."

Noisily clearing his throat, Dylan paced away from her, leaving Grace wondering if he was going to walk off in the middle of their intense exchange. Instead he turned. And as he did she noticed the pathos in his gaze, the moisture that made his dark eyes glisten like agate.

"I know you hate me enough to want your freedom and I don't blame you, Grace. I know you'll never forget the mistakes I've made. I also know I deserve all the punishment life deals out. All I ask is that you believe I'm trying to make amends and make some effort to accept me the way I am now." He raked his fingers through his hair. "It won't be easy. I know that."

She hesitated. Studied him. Judged him sincere. Her voice was soft, her inflection heartfelt, when she said, "No, it won't be."

Left unspoken was any promise to try to understand the man she'd once loved enough to marry and start a family with. This current version of Dylan was closer to that original person than he had been for years. Did she dare open her heart again?

Logic told her no, while her emotions urged forgiveness. For the present she chose to heed her sensible side. If Dylan continued to be this kind of appealing person, then perhaps she would eventually reconsider. They had time. At least she hoped they did.

That was the real question, wasn't it? Were they living on borrowed time or were they going to actually have a chance to get to know each other again, to perhaps pull their fractured marriage back together?

Grace's follow-up question depended more on her than on her estranged husband. She silently asked herself, *Do I want to go back to the way our life was?* and answered easily that she did not.

She assumed she'd eventually be able to forgive Dylan, up to a point, but she never wanted to return to the days when his whole focus had been on making lots of money. Back then, he'd barely had time for her or the children. He hadn't even bothered to pretend interest in their daily lives, let alone accompany them anywhere unless he absolutely had to.

Grace sighed, letting out a noisy whoosh of air and shaking her head sadly. Even Sunday mornings, when he was free of work responsibilities, he usually opted to stay home while she took the kids to Sunday school by herself.

Which reminded her that it was currently Saturday. Were they allowed to find a nearby church and attend, or was that another privilege now denied them?

Thoughtful, she glanced from her husband to the hall table. The large manila envelope with files the marshal had left was still there, unopened.

"I'm going to go sit down with those instructions and memorize as much as I can," she said flatly, gesturing. "Do you want to stay here and look at them after I'm finished, or would you like to come over to my side of the house and do it with me?"

"Did I just get invited to cross the border into enemy territory?" He looked as though he was blushing.

Grace had to smile in spite of herself. "If your passport is in order and you have a current visa, I guess you'll be okay."

His grin matched then surpassed hers. "I'm sure I have proper documentation for any circumstance," he joked. "The U.S. marshals think of everything."

Although she made a face at him, she wasn't really angry. This kind of humorous, witty exchange had been one of the things she'd once found so appealing about Dylan. He'd had a mischievous bent that had so well meshed with hers that they could anticipate the twists in each other's funny quips almost instantly. In short, Dylan *got her.* At least that was the way it had been when they were dating and he was finishing law school.

Those were halcyon days, Grace admitted. And, in her heart of hearts, she truly did miss them.

Glancing at her soon-to-be-ex she swallowed hard. She'd missed experiencing this playful side of Dylan. It was delightful to see him as someone who could find humor in almost any situation and be comfortable in his own skin the way he was now. Instead of his normal business attire he was clad in worn jeans and had chosen a long-sleeved shirt that hid the bandage on his arm. His dark hair was mussed, his chin slightly shadowed by stubble. He would never have gone even one day without shaving when they were in St. Louis. Now, he looked more like the reality television version of middle America than he did a high-powered lawyer.

That will change, Grace warned herself. *As soon as he's testified and gone back to his former career, he'll be just the way he was when I filed for divorce.*

Except... She glanced at his arm and noticed blood spotting his sleeve. "You must have hurt yourself when you fell," she said, pointing.

"It's nothing. Just bumped the place where I was shot when I took that dive."

Looping a hand through his good arm, she led him to her part of the house, through her sparsely furnished living room and down the hallway to the bath before positioning him at the edge of the tub and ordering, "Sit. I found a first-aid kit. I'll redo the bandage for you."

"That's really not necessary."

Grace stood her ground. "Oh, yes, it is. Unless you plan to explain to the neighbors why you have a bleeding bullet hole in your arm."

"Point taken," Dylan said, assuming a seated position balancing on the narrow rim of the tub and rolling up his sleeve. "Do we have a washing machine or are you going to have to beat the clothes on a rock in a river?"

"We have a washing machine. And a dryer. Right uptown, aren't we?"

Dylan sobered and held out his arm for her. "I'm so sorry, Gracie."

She thought about chastising him for using the nickname again, then changed her mind. The man was bleeding. The least she could do was to allow him a little latitude.

Her fingers gently removed and discarded the previous bandage. It was hard to look at the hole piercing his arm without wincing. Not only was it reddened, there was a nasty bruise surrounding the injury, as if he had been hit with a baseball bat after being shot. Although he wasn't complaining, she knew it must hurt. A lot.

"I'll try to be gentle," she said, filled with trepidation and moving slowly, deliberately.

The sight of Dylan's wound was doing funny things to her equilibrium and making her wish she had not insisted on doctoring him. It was the thought that the bullet could have ended his life that was tearing her up inside. Instead of changing a bandage, she could just as easily be arranging his funeral.

This relocation *had* to work, she reminded herself sternly. Because if it failed and they were tracked down, Dylan would very likely die. And that would kill a part of her heart and soul as surely as if she'd shared his fate.

Dylan couldn't take his eyes off his wife. Although her slim fingers were trembling and beads of sweat were glistening on her forehead, she persevered. He'd always known she was an extraordinary woman but her strength and resilience during this current ordeal was absolutely magnificent. The worst aspect of that realization, for him, was knowing he didn't dare tell her how much he admired her. Not yet, at any rate.

Their questionable future was one of the things stopping him. Dylan was far from certain that he would live through this dire testing of his wisdom and his spirit. Therefore, if he did coax Grace into forgiving him enough to want to try again, she might be hurt even worse in the long run. The best thing for everyone concerned was to maintain the status quo; Grace and the children must be kept separate from him as much as humanly possible until they were all in the clear. Or until he was out of the picture for good.

Thoughts of permanently parting from this tenderhearted woman were painful, poignant. They hurt him far more than the wound in his arm. And were going to be harder to see healed, too, he imagined.

As Grace finished taping the dressing and backed away, Dylan looked up at her. "You do understand why I was so cross with you for leaving the kids alone, don't you?"

She nodded and pressed her lips into a thin line before answering. "Yes. I didn't stop to think the attack on you might have been a diversion. Actually, it was good that nothing bad happened because it served as a warning. I'll be more suspicious from now on."

"That's my girl."

The moment the carelessly spoken words were out of his mouth, Dylan knew he'd made another big mistake. Rather than stay long enough for Grace to react negatively, he quickly left the room and headed for the kitchen where she had placed the file they were planning to study.

She followed. Although she didn't chastise him, there was a definite chill in the air that had not been there earlier.

"All right," Grace said, choosing a chair directly across the table from him. "Let's get started."

When he opened the folder, Dylan found three sections. One was his, one hers and the third pertained to their children, primarily the older two. Grace claimed all but Dylan's and arrayed their contents in front of her.

"It says here that the kids still have a month of school before summer vacation starts. That's going to go over like a lead balloon."

Dylan chuckled. "Beth will like the idea. Kyle, maybe not so much."

She made a face and drawled, "You think?"

"Yup. He's going to be ecstatic."

"Yeah, right. It also says they're both enrolled in the gifted and talented program so they already have some after-school activities scheduled."

"That's probably good. It'll keep them occupied and maybe they can make a few friends before school is out for the summer."

"Do we want them to?"

"For their sakes, I assume so," he replied. "We can't keep them locked in the house all the time and make our family seem normal at the same time."

Her eyebrows shot up. "Normal?"

"I didn't say we *were* normal, I just meant we need to look the part."

"Okay. I suppose that does make sense."

Dylan reached for her hand and laid his over it. "Grace, I…"

She withdrew. "If you're planning to apologize again, save it. We all know you're sorry and we all know you wish you could go back and do everything differently. I've got it, Dylan. Dwelling on your faults isn't getting us anywhere. We need to stick with these files until we know them forward and backward, then start testing the kids to make sure they understand everything, too."

Nodding soberly, he sat back in his chair and cradled his arm. "It says here that I start orientation at work first thing Monday morning." He used his good hand to display the set of keys Marshal Trier had given him. "These are for the house, as you already know, and for a car. We're now the proud owners of our very own reconditioned minivan."

When he saw her jaw drop, he had to laugh. "I imagine it gets better mileage than the fancy SUV you left behind."

"One car? That's it? That's all?"

Dylan made a show of inspecting his file and even shook it as if he expected more keys to fall out. "Looks like it. You'll have to drive me to work and drop me off if you want to keep the wheels for yourself."

The grimace she shot his way was contrite and comical. "I thought it couldn't get any worse but it has. I not only am a soccer mom, I now have to look like one!"

With so much tension in the family and not long in which to coach the children on their new backgrounds, Grace decided it would be too chancy to go to church that Sunday and mingle with strangers. Instead they spent the day getting used to the house and setting rules about what was and wasn't acceptable in their reconstructed lives.

"I made a serious mistake yesterday," she told her family as they unwrapped and distributed a take-out supper of burgers and fries that same evening. "When I thought your daddy had been hurt, I ran over to see. I shouldn't have left you kids alone like that."

"I can take care of Beth and Brandon," Kyle insisted, staring at his father as if Dylan were an adversary.

It was the boy's changeable moods that worried Grace the most. One minute Kyle was happy to see his dad and the next he was acting as if he wished Dylan would go away again. She supposed it was natural for the children to be confused and to act out, at least until they began to feel secure again. All her children would be safer with the big brother of the family on guard. Kyle might not be able to do much if there was an attack, but at least he'd be alert.

It had occurred to Grace to take the eldest child aside and have a private talk with him about their situation. Instead, Dylan sent the other two out into the fenced backyard to play and spoke up himself.

Her insides began to flutter while her outward persona remained stoic. Hearing Dylan express his innermost concerns was more unnerving than thinking about her own.

"There are still plenty of bad guys running around wanting to shut me up," Dylan said in conclusion. "That's why we moved and why we have to hide this way."

"I hate it here," Kyle muttered. "This house is lame and the people are worse. None of the kids I saw even have decent bikes."

Grace was flabbergasted. Her son was the image of his father, all right, complete with Dylan's social-climbing attitudes and focus on possessions. Come to think of it, she'd sounded like a snob, too, when she'd been discussing the minivan.

She raised a hand as if asking for the floor at a meeting, then spoke without waiting for permission. "In case you haven't noticed, Kyle, you don't have a fancy bike anymore, either. And I don't drive a luxury SUV. Maybe someday we can get those things back, but for the time being, this is how it is. Got that?"

The glare he turned on her was even more irate than the one he'd recently used on his father.

Grace refused to back down or to make excuses. "I don't like this situation any more than anybody else does, but that doesn't change it one bit. You, and the rest of us, are going to have to accept what's happened and live with it." Lowering her voice, she added, "Or we're all going to be in deep trouble. Do I make myself clear?"

"Yeah."

She knew she could have stopped the boy with a harsh word when he rose and stormed from the room. Instead she let him go so he'd have a chance to cool off.

Dylan leaned back in his chair and shook his head. "Well, that didn't go very well."

"He'll come around eventually. You'll see. This is all too new for any of us to settle down yet. What do you say we fire up the old van and cruise by the school and your new job so we can find them easily tomorrow morning?"

"I don't know if it's a good idea to leave the house for no reason. We can set the GPS to find them when we need to."

Grace laughed, waiting for her husband to realize what he'd just said. Finally she put an end to his puzzled expression by saying, "What GPS, Mr. Appleby? We have cheap burner phones with no whistles and bells, and I doubt very much if the car they gave us has those nice accessories, either."

"We've been returned to the dark ages," Dylan said with a blossoming grin. "No wonder Kyle is so bummed."

EIGHT

Dylan had been positive he wouldn't sleep well and was surprised to find the opposite happening. Not only did he nod off almost immediately, he didn't awaken on Monday morning until he heard familiar household noises.

He went to join the others. "Morning. Something sure smells good. Did you all sleep well?" Dylan asked with a welcoming grin as he raked his fingers through his short, dark hair and yawned.

"Fine," Grace replied. She gestured at the table where their children were already eating. "Since you're here, I suppose you may as well pull up a chair. We'll have to leave soon, you know."

"Um. Don't remind me. I have orientation today."

It was oddly comforting to hear Grace ask, "Are you sure you're up to it?"

"I'm okay. Nobody will suspect my arm is messed up."

"That's exactly my point. If you don't tell your new bosses what's wrong, you may be asked to do things that hurt you."

"Well, since the marshals got me this job, I'm assuming somebody at work knows enough to cut me some slack. If not, I'll just do what I have to do." He paused for a sip of hot coffee before adding, "Like we all will."

When Grace didn't comment further, Dylan took a place at the table and helped Brandon cut his pancakes into bite-size pieces. By the time the meal was over, they were almost out of time.

Observing his family gathering their possessions and heading for the garage, he could see that they were all pretty nervous. So was he. It had been a long time since he'd had a job that required physical labor and he wondered if he was capable of switching gears like that. Oh, he was strong enough and in good health except for his arm, but his mind was always spinning, always thinking up better ways to do things, so he'd have to be careful. It was one thing to be the new guy on the job and quite another to waltz in and try to reorganize the business.

That notion made him smile, then quickly sober. Too bad he hadn't used more caution when he'd been asked to push those adoptions through. He'd convinced himself he was acting for the benefit of babies who'd had no homes. If he'd stopped to really consider, to question the validity of some of those claims, he'd have realized he was in the wrong. Sincere motives to do good didn't count when a person broke the law. Black and white was not supposed to blur into a fog of gray that obscured the truth.

Dylan stepped ahead of Grace and placed himself at the front door like a sentinel. "Wait. Let me go first and open the garage before you bring the kids out."

"Why don't we use the side door?" She scowled.

"Because the overhead is padlocked and has to be opened from the outside. Besides, it's smart to be cautious," he explained, trying to sound nonchalant when he felt as nervous as he would have if he'd spotted hungry, man-eating lions lurking in the untrimmed shrubbery.

"Okay. We'll stay right here until you tell us it's safe." She bent to lift Brandon into her arms on the side opposite the strap of her shoulder bag.

Dylan saw Kyle sidle past his mother and come after him. "I said, everybody needs to wait inside."

The boy didn't slow until he reached his father's side in spite of Grace's shout for him to stop.

"You heard your mother." Dylan said.

"Yeah, but I figured you'd have trouble lifting that door with one arm messed up," Kyle countered logically. "I came to help you."

"I hate it when you're more sensible than I am," Dylan quipped, ruffling the boy's red hair affectionately. "Okay. I'll undo the padlock and you can lift with me."

Even with Kyle's help the door was difficult to handle. It was old and heavy, made of solid wood instead of modern, lightweight aluminum. If it had not been constructed in two sections, one for each parking space, it would have been unmanageable.

When Dylan finally laid eyes on the brown minivan he almost laughed out loud. Grace was going to pitch a fit. He figured he had better not give voice to any amusement or it would make the situation a whole lot worse.

"Whoa, Dad, what is that thing?"

"It's an old Ford but I'm not positive what model." He approached the vehicle slowly, hardly able to believe this was to be their sole transportation.

"Can we come out now?" Grace called from the porch.

"Sure."

The sight of the dilapidated van had distracted Dylan enough that he had unknowingly relaxed his guard. The sound of a loud engine rumbling in the distance snapped him out of it.

Instead of waiting for the rest of his family to join him, he hurried back to Grace, slipped his good arm around her and hustled her into the musty-smelling garage.

Her eyes were wide when they met his. "What's wrong?"

"I don't know," Dylan explained. "I just heard something that spooked me and realized I wasn't paying close enough attention."

"That's because we can only stay on high alert for so long before we shut down," Grace offered. "I've noticed that the more scared I am in the beginning, the bigger the letdown at the end."

He kept his arm around her and tugged her into the shadows as the rattling, revving sound drew nearer and nearer.

Grace leaned against Dylan as if she'd forgotten to be standoffish. When the motorcycle that was causing the roar cruised past, she gasped. "Isn't that the same...?"

"Looks like it."

He was about to reassure her that the rider probably lived nearby and was therefore no threat when the man turned the reflective faceplate of his helmet toward them.

Dylan didn't have to actually see his eyes to know the rider was staring right at them. The cycle slowed, its powerful engine putt-putting instead of whining the way a smaller bike would.

Freezing in place, Dylan wondered if this was the end already. Had they been located this soon, this easily? The hair on the back of his neck prickled. He shoved Grace behind him and took a step forward.

The rider managed to balance as the motorcycle nearly came to a complete stop. Then he raised his hand, pointed his index finger toward Dylan and bent his thumb with a quick jerk before laughing raucously and racing away.

Dylan didn't know anything about the man or why he'd apparently singled them out for harassment—if that's all it was. The only thing he was positive of was that the helmeted figure had been pantomiming shooting a pistol. At the newly christened Appleby family.

Grace was the first to break and make a beeline for the van. She fastened Brandon in a booster seat before sliding behind the wheel and letting Dylan do the rest. To her surprise, the old vehicle not only started easily, it purred as if it were new.

The maps in the marshal's instruction packet showed that the warehouse store where Dylan was employed was on the way to the children's school, so that would be their first stop. She let the dented, brown minivan idle in the driveway while Dylan closed and relocked the garage door.

"I thought you'd pitch a fit when you saw this van," he commented, joining her.

"I didn't have time to get upset. Who do you think that guy on the motorcycle was?"

"I don't know. I didn't get a look at his license plate, did you?"

"No. It was too small to see from the garage. The next time he drives by I'm going to be ready. Do we happen to have binoculars? I didn't come across any."

"Not that I know of," Dylan answered, "but I can check at work and see if the store sells them. I understand their stock is impressive, everything from groceries to TV sets to lawnmowers."

"Well, I don't think we'll need to mow that stubble in the yard for a while, not as dry as it's apparently been around here this spring."

"I know. It looks parched compared to home."

"Really? I thought we came from Arizona, *John*."

"Right." He looked contrite. "You're absolutely right. We need to stay in character all the time or one of us is liable to slip and ruin the whole setup."

"You kids remember that, too," Grace cautioned as she drove the unfamiliar streets, hoping she'd be able to find her way home after dropping off her husband and the older children. She had never had the innate sense of direction that her husband seemed to be endowed with. If familiar landmarks happened to change since the last time she'd been somewhere, she could very easily become disoriented.

Dylan leaned forward in the passenger seat and pointed out the window. "There's the store sign. Whoa. It is a big place."

"I've heard their merchandise is top-notch," Grace told him. "I'll be back for you at five. Right?"

"Right. And I won't have to worry about lunch. They sell their own brand of hot dogs and soda inside, supposedly at cost."

Grace couldn't help chuckling softly. "You have gone native, haven't you…John?"

"When in Rome," he quipped, stepping down and slamming the door. "Be careful today."

"Always."

Watching him turn and walk away, Grace was suddenly overcome with a surge of pride she had not anticipated. Dylan was a capable attorney with several college degrees, yet he was approaching this new phase of his life with the kind of enthusiasm and courage she hadn't seen from him in years.

In moments she was able to banish most of those tender, appreciative feelings. Most. Not all. She knew it was foolish to let herself look up to this man after all he'd done, yet there was no denying that his character had recently taken a turn for the better.

She checked the traffic behind her and to both sides as she turned down a nearby alley. In a crowded parking lot like this one, there was no way to anticipate an attack the way they could when at home. And yet, the motorcyclist had still managed to sideswipe Dylan.

Picturing that reflective helmet visor and imagining the evil stare hidden behind it, Grace shuddered.

She and Brandon were going to have to go home eventually. And when they did, she planned to make a dash for the house and recheck the locks on all the doors and windows. There was nothing wrong with a little sensible paranoia when you *knew* somebody was after you.

Dylan's concerns about work had been for nothing. Once he'd been given a personally conducted tour of the store he was assigned to forklift duty, a task he could manage pretty well one-handed due to the assist knob on the steering wheel. He figured, as long as he took his time and didn't go racing around on the thing, he'd be okay. By lunchtime he'd mastered the lift levers so well he was actually keeping up with the younger, crew-cut coworker who had been assigned to teach him the ropes.

One additional thing the marshals had warned about was getting too friendly with people who might inadvertently reveal your idiosyncrasies. That made perfect sense to Dylan, which is why he chose to eat lunch alone, outside on a bench near the loading dock. Trucks came and went as he sat there thinking and wondering about his family while a few other employees stood around smoking and talking in small groups.

Finally his imagination had caused him so much grief he decided to break down and call Grace. The only phones they had were the ones they'd been given and there were only two numbers in the contact file; his wife's and the marshals'.

When Grace answered there was a tremor in her voice. "H-hello?"

"It's me," Dylan said.

"You scared me to death!"

"Sorry. I'm on lunch break and I wanted to check on you. How's it going? Did you get the kids to school okay?"

"It was fine. The people in the office treated us like VIPs. Are you sure they don't know our situation?"

"That's just regular Southern hospitality," Dylan told her with a quiet chuckle. "The guys I work with are great, too." He laughed again. "They can be a little hard to understand sometimes."

"I know what you mean," Grace said. "I had to really work to decipher what the school secretary was saying. It's a good thing they didn't tell us to say we were from Georgia or Alabama or one of those states."

"I'm sure that's all taken into consideration."

"Right." There was a hesitation in her reply that grew into a long pause.

"Grace?"

"Mary Grace, to you," she told him sternly. "Where are you, exactly? Can anybody overhear you?"

"Not with all the noise of trucks unloading."

"Okay. Just don't forget again."

"Yes, ma'am." He drawled his reply into four syllables to mimic a Texas accent.

"Keep that up and I'll have to buy you a Stetson for your birthday," Grace teased.

Dylan's heart skipped several beats. His birthday was in the fall, almost six months away. Was that Grace's subtle way of promising they'd still be together?

"Unless you're wearing prison stripes by that time," she added, sounding a lot less amused than she had previously.

"I think the standard jumpsuit is orange, only not nearly as pretty as your hair," Dylan replied. "Are you really all right? No more problems?"

"None. It's been quiet since Brandon and I got home."

"When do you have to go get the other kids?"

"At three for Beth and three-thirty for Kyle. I figured to park myself in the office and wait there, at least for a few days, until we can set up a schedule that suits everybody."

"Be careful you don't chat too much," he warned.

"Hey, you're the one using the wrong names, not me."

He had to concede the point. "Okay, you win. Just check

the street carefully from inside the house before you step out, will you? Promise?"

"Have you had more problems?" she asked.

Dylan shook his head. "No. Not yet, anyway. I imagine, if there was real trouble, it would hit us before we were aware of any danger."

His jaw clenched when his wife said, "Yeah. That's what I'm afraid of," and bid him a terse goodbye.

She was right. They could be in terrible jeopardy before they even noticed. That was why the Witness Protection Program was so necessary.

It was also why they had to be on guard every waking moment. Undoubtedly powerful people already knew what a danger Dylan's testimony would be to their positions, not to mention the very good chance that they'd end up in prison as a result of his inside information.

These people had to be influential as well as malevolent or they never would have been able to outwit the authorities and maintain such a lucrative business.

Some business, he mused. They had systematically ruined lives—and he had helped them do it. That was the hardest, most personally painful fact he'd had to acknowledge. Still, those events had brought him here, to a new life and perhaps even to the salvaging of his broken marriage.

Was that *fair?* he wondered. Shouldn't he be facing punishment instead of seeing rainbows behind the rain? Was he really forgiven the way the Bible claimed was possible?

Time would tell. There had already been negative consequences from his former actions and there would undoubtedly be more to come. As Dylan saw it, his penance was going to be served when he stood up in court and helped put kidnappers and baby stealers behind bars, hopefully with long, long sentences to keep them there.

And in the meantime? He got to his feet, dumped his trash in a nearby rubbish can and headed back to work.

In the meantime all he had to do was to carefully pretend to be a regular working guy with no bounty on his head.

He gave a wry smile and mumbled, "Piece of cake," while continuing to scan his surroundings for would-be assassins and wondering if he'd ever feel safe again.

NINE

As the first week passed, then the second, Grace began to fall into a fairly comfortable routine. The children seemed happy enough, considering, and to her shock, Dylan actually acted as if he was enjoying his new lifestyle.

She wished she could say the same. It had been a long time since she'd had to keep house by herself and the rear yard was such a mess she hated to allow the kids to play out there. They didn't seem to notice the difference between this place and the manicured lawn, neat ornamental shrubs and lovely blooms they'd had surrounding their home in Missouri, but Grace certainly did. This backyard had only one good thing going for it. It was fenced. Other than that there was no comparison.

The first few days in Houston she'd kept busy organizing the house and memorizing various routes she could travel when picking up Dylan and the children. Nobody had cautioned her to avoid being too predictable but it seemed logical to make random changes and choose alternate paths to and from her daily destinations.

Nevertheless, the days began to drag by and Grace found herself wishing that school would soon be out so she'd have more than little Brandon's company during the long summer days. To her dismay, she was actually looking forward to hearing the kids squabbling!

Dylan had promised to accompany her to the end-of-the-

year concert and awards ceremony in which their two eldest
were to perform this coming Friday evening. If he had not
agreed to go, Grace wasn't certain she'd have wanted to
attend. She still left the house with trepidation every day
and, like a wise old mama cat who kept moving her vulnerable newborn kittens, she didn't relax until she had her
whole family in one place again.

The most sensible arrangement was to wait for Dylan
in the store's parking lot for about an hour every weekday
instead of going home after she picked up the kids. She'd
quickly found a cool, breezy spot where she could watch
the loading dock and see him the instant he appeared. Hot
Texas afternoons made the wait tedious. This one was no
exception.

"I wanna wear my pink Sunday dress on Friday," Beth
announced as Grace pulled up and stopped in their familiar, shady spot.

"Your teacher said you should have on a white blouse
and dark skirt or slacks so all of you will look the same."

"But I want the *pink* dress."

Grace figured this was as good a time as any to remind
the girl that she no longer owned the fancy dress. "Beth,
honey, we left those clothes behind. Remember?"

"Yeah, like my BMX bike," her older brother grumbled,
making a sour face.

"And my whole house and almost everything I loved,
too," Grace said, regretting her brusqueness. "So knock it
off. Both of you."

She might have said more if she hadn't been distracted
by a revving engine. The power-packed sound was coming
from near the rear of the store. Then, suddenly, a low-slung,
red muscle car fishtailed out from behind a semitrailer and
headed straight for her.

Grace tensed. She had only seconds in which to react.

Frantic, she turned the key in the ignition. The engine coughed. Died. "Come on, come on."

The van started on the second try. Grace slammed it into reverse. Floored the gas and manhandled the wheel to swerve behind a heavy cement base that supported one of the store's massive, overhead light poles.

The powerful car roared past them, missing one corner of her front bumper by mere inches.

"Whoa, nice driving Mom!" Kyle was beaming and bouncing up and down on his knees on the seat.

If she hadn't been so shocked and frightened she might have appreciated his compliment a lot more.

Who or what was *that?* Were they showing off or was their behavior much more ominous?

Grace let the van idle and clenched her jaw while she eyed the far reaches of the busy parking lot. Dylan had been right. With so many variables and unknowns, an attacker could be on them before they even knew he was coming.

That conclusion was more than sobering. It was chilling. Especially right now when her heart felt as though it was about to pound its way out of her chest.

Dylan had to admit he was tired by late afternoon. He'd managed to keep up with the other warehousemen but he felt every one of his thirty-two years near the end of his shift. There was a lot to be said for genuine physical labor, he mused, picturing himself working out at his athletic club and realizing that his body-building routine had not begun to match the daily rigors of this job.

He'd moved the last bin on his list and was sitting in an aisle aboard the forklift, taking a well-earned break before receiving another assignment. Earphones connected him into the router who kept inventory and made certain that customers of the warehouse store were never disappointed by spotty merchandise distribution.

Some of the others on his crew had stepped outside for a smoke while his partner, Mac, had popped over to the snack bar for a soda.

Dylan yawned. Stretched. Decided to stand for a moment to try to work kinks out of his muscles.

Raising both arms overhead he thrust them as high as he could and took a deep breath. Glanced toward the high ceiling. Saw slight movement out of the corner of his eye.

Someone in the distance shouted, "John!"

In the split second it took Dylan to realize that the warning was meant for him, he saw a stack of cardboard boxes on the top shelf start to move.

They teetered for a moment, then passed their center of gravity and began to fall as if in slow motion.

Dylan was directly below them, hemmed in on one side by aisles of merchandise and on the other by the forklift. There was no time to run.

Acting solely on instinct he leaped toward the largest box on the floor beside him, crashed against its side and plummeted in through the wide-open top like an Olympic swimmer entering a pool for a race.

Several of the heavy cases of canned goods careened off the sides of the lift and followed him into the enormous container of softer merchandise.

Dylan had the breath knocked out of him.

Lying still and wondering how the full boxes on the top shelf could possibly have fallen, he took inventory of his body, pleased to note that he was all in one piece.

At least he hoped so.

Grace had barely regained her composure after the near miss in the parking lot when her cell phone startled her anew. Her hands were shaking as she dug it out of her purse. Dylan had made it a habit to call during his lunch break but it was far too late in the afternoon for that. He'd be clocking out in a little more than an hour and the only others who had her number were the kids' teachers.

"Hello?" She had to clamp her free hand over her other ear to mute the children's whiny voices. "I'm sorry. What? I don't think I heard correctly."

"I said, can you come to the store as soon as possible, Mrs. Appleby? There's been a slight accident. We'd like to send your husband to the hospital to be checked out but he's refusing treatment. Maybe if you ask him, he'll agree to go."

Eyes wide, insides roiling, Grace slipped the van into drive. "I'm already here. Shall I pull up to the loading dock or come in the front door?"

"The dock will be fine, ma'am. I'll watch for you."

"Okay." With the slim little cell phone pressed between her ear and shoulder, she wheeled into an open spot next to the elevated platform for the loading dock and screeched to a halt. "I'm here."

"Good. We'll be right out."

All the children had sensed her anxiety and were clamoring for answers. Grace focused on Kyle. "You're in charge. I'm going to leave the car running to keep you cool. Lock the doors and keep the windows rolled up most of the way. Understand? Don't touch anything else and see that you don't open the doors until I get back with your father."

The boy scrambled over the back of the passenger seat and slid into the place usually reserved for Dylan. "Is Dad okay?"

Grace fisted the phone and passed it to the boy. "I don't know. The man who called said they're sending him home, so it can't be too bad." She got out, slammed the door and pointed to the locks. To her relief, Kyle and Beth both followed directions.

Wheeling, Grace hurried up a concrete stairway, one palm sliding up the metal railing. Her body shook, her heart hammering so hard she could feel her pulse behind her eyes and in her temples. Her worst fears had always been for Dylan's safety. Now, they had been realized.

The moment she saw him walking toward her she was so relieved she had to grab the railing for a moment to keep her balance. A young man wearing the same light orange vest that designated all the store's employees had hold of Dylan's elbow and seemed to be guiding him.

Grace didn't hesitate to step directly in front of her husband and cup his face in both hands. His cheeks were flushed but his eyes seemed to focus well, although there was mistiness to his gaze.

His hands closed around her wrists. Nobody moved.

Finally he said, "I'm okay, Mary Grace. It was just a little accident."

"What happened?"

"I'll tell you on the way home." Turning her bodily, he slipped an arm around her shoulders and bid his coworker a brief, casual goodbye. "See you tomorrow, Mac."

"Only if your head's on straight by then," the crew-cut young man countered with a grin. "You know what the boss said."

"Yeah, yeah." Nodding and guiding his wife back through the door, Dylan increased his pace.

"What is it?" Grace asked. "Why are we in such a hurry?"

"Because you and the kids are too exposed while you're here. And because I'm not totally sure what happened to me today."

She signaled to Kyle to unlock the van doors and slid behind the wheel while Dylan took over the front passenger seat.

They had merged into heavy, afternoon traffic before she started to question him further. "Okay. Let's have it. What's going on and why did you say you didn't know what had happened to you? Were you unconscious or something?"

"I sure could have been," Dylan replied with a grimace. "I was doing my job and minding my own business. The next thing I knew, Mac and a couple of other guys were yelling and there was a stack of merchandise falling over on top of me."

"You weren't hurt? Honestly?"

"Honestly, although I should have been. The cases that fell had been piled high on an upper shelf and were packed with canned goods. As heavy as they were, I should have ended up with a concussion, or worse."

"What saved you?"

"Teddy bears."

Grace snapped a glance his way. "Teddy bears?"

Smiling, Dylan nodded. "Yup. Great big stuffed ones, taller than Brandon and real fluffy. I dived into a big bin full of them when I saw the stack of cases swaying and starting to fall. By the time the avalanche was over, I was buried, all right, but some of the bears were between me and a world of hurt."

"That's amazing."

"I thought so, too." His smile faded and he leaned closer to whisper to her, "You haven't broken the rules and called your mother, have you?"

"Of course not. I was told she could lose her nest egg if I did."

"Okay."

When he shrugged, Grace saw him wince. He might not have received life-threatening injuries but he was still banged up. "How about your arm?" she asked. "Did you hurt it again?"

He displayed and moved it to demonstrate. "Nope. Almost good as new. Didn't even disturb the little bandage I stuck on it this morning."

"That's a plus, at least." She knew she had the steering wheel in a punishing grip but her nerves refused to let her relax. "I don't think you should go back to work there, Dylan. Not after today."

"Don't be silly. I'll give the marshals a call tonight and advise them, as we'd promised, but I don't intend to quit over what was probably just an accident."

"Probably?" Grace made a dour face. "If it's at all likely that the falling cases were aimed at you, you have to walk away. While you still can."

He huffed and started to smile more broadly. "No. Not yet. It might surprise you to know I actually enjoy going to work there and not having to sit behind a desk or face judges and juries."

"You're happy? Like this? Having to wonder if the next stranger you pass might turn around and try to kill you? What kind of life is that?"

"Right now it's mine and I've decided I might as well own it," Dylan said, ending with a noisy exhale.

All Grace could do was sit there, stunned, and force herself to concentrate on her driving while her emotions roiled and seethed. The man was impossible! Initially he'd acted as if his sins were justifiable. Now he was accepting dire threats as though they were inevitable. Did he think he deserved to die? Was that what had scrambled his thought processes?

"That does it. You do need your head examined. I'm taking you to the emergency room."

Dylan's strong grip around her closest wrist was startling. So was his guttural "No."

"Give me one good reason why not. Just one."

"Okay. Because anybody who wants to find us may be able to hack into electronic medical records. And that's just the beginning. Would you like to hear more options?"

She failed to come up with a clever retort. There was a good chance Dylan was right, at least in part. Or maybe it had already happened. If they'd been tracked down and she failed to tell him about the incident in the parking lot, it could make things even worse.

"You can let go of my wrist," Grace said, resigned to confessing the near miss. "Something else happened today, too. While I was waiting for you to get off work, an idiot in a hot rod almost took out the van."

"What! Where were you?"

"Same place I always am after I pick up the kids. That's probably a mistake, I know, but there's so little shade I didn't see the harm."

"Are you sure he targeted you?"

"No. The only thing I'm positive about is that he missed us."

"Mom drove like a race car driver." Kyle piped up from the backseat. "It was so fun."

Dylan was shaking his head. "All right. Let's go home. If our contact advises me to quit my job, I will."

"And we're telling the marshals about both near misses," Grace insisted. "That way, if you take a turn for the worse due to some hidden damage, I can call paramedics without breaking any rules. Which reminds me," she added, picking up her phone. "There must be something wrong with the battery in this thing. I noticed it was almost dead when your boss called me a few minutes ago. I know I had it plugged into the charger all night."

"You haven't used it much since then?"

"Only to talk to you during lunch," Grace said.

She saw her husband carefully studying the screen that showed usage, battery life and stored numbers. Then he took his cell out and compared them.

"You sure you haven't used this for anything else?"

"I did call St. George Place Elementary to double check the times for after-school activities. Why?"

Dylan displayed the two phones side by side. "Assuming

we started out with an equal number of available minutes, you've used a lot more than I have."

"Maybe the music teacher talked longer than I thought," Grace explained. "I contacted her to confirm what the kids needed to wear to the recital."

"That must be it. It's this coming Friday night, right?"

"Yes. The program starts at six. You're still going, aren't you?"

"Wouldn't miss it," he said with a smile in his voice.

Grace used the rearview mirror to check on her passengers, assuming they'd be delighted to hear that their father was going to come through for them.

Brandon had nodded off in his booster seat, his head flopped to one side. Beth was curled up in the far corner with her nose in a book. And Kyle? Kyle was staring at his father's back as if he'd just discovered that Dylan was really the boogeyman in disguise.

Grace made a face. *Terrific.*

TEN

The more Dylan mulled over the details of their so-called accidents, the more he was certain they'd been targeted, so that was the way he decided to report the incidents.

His call was answered on the second ring.

"McCall's office."

"Marshal McCall, this is Dylan—I mean John Appleby."

"McCall's out in the field," the voice on the phone said. "But I know who you are. This is Burke Trier. I escorted you to Houston. What's up? Problems?"

"Maybe," Dylan said. "There were two suspicious accidents today." He went through the stories, step by step, concluding with, "There's one detail that really bothers me and makes me more suspicious."

"Go ahead," the marshal said evenly.

"It was the way the shipment came apart when it fell on me. We don't remove the plastic wrapping around each pallet of goods until we're done shifting them. Those cases should have been held together so they couldn't possibly tumble down the way they did."

"It's not the first time something like that has happened, I'm sure. Did you ask about it?"

"Up to a point," Dylan said. "I didn't want to sound paranoid or come across as a disgruntled employee thinking of suing the store. You guys said to keep a low profile."

"Right. Well done," the marshal told him. "And nobody was hurt?"

"No. The only damage inside was some dented cans and busted-open cardboard cartons. Grace was able to out-maneuver the reckless driver. He never touched the van."

"In that case I wouldn't worry, Mr. Appleby," Trier said. "I'll advise Summers and McCall about the incidents but I don't expect them to suggest any changes in your placement at this time. Just keep your wits about you and call again if you find out that somebody actually has it in for you."

Dylan heard a soft chuckle before the marshal added, "You haven't made any of your coworkers mad, have you?"

"Not that I know of. Although there is a motorcyclist in my neighborhood who seems to have a chip on his shoulder where I'm concerned. He almost ran me down right after we moved in."

"Is he harassing you?"

"Not anymore," Dylan explained, raking his fingers through his tousled hair and sweeping it back. "Come to think of it, we haven't seen him in a week or so."

"Sounds like normal suburban life to me." He chuckled more noticeably. "Tell you what, the next time you see something that bothers you, get all the details you can and write them down so you won't forget. If you start to see a pattern instead of coincidences, McCall will want to know."

"All right. Thanks."

Dylan ended the call and turned around to find Grace watching. She had obviously been listening, too.

"What did they say?" she asked, frowning.

"That both were probably accidents."

"But you're not so sure, are you? I can see it in your face."

"I'm not totally convinced, no. The cases that fell should have been wrapped together and secured to the pallet with heavy plastic. One of the first things I was taught was to never raise an unwrapped load too high."

"Maybe the plastic tore."

"You have to cut it with a razor knife to get it off, and even then it clings to all the square corners. I can't see how it could have just fallen off."

"So, maybe one of the guys you work with goofed. He made the mistake of loosening the wrappings, then discovered he was supposed to stack the load for storage instead of delivering it to the floor. He didn't want to get in trouble, so he went ahead in spite of the safety rules. Isn't that a likely scenario?"

"Actually, it is. We have a few younger guys who are a couple steers short of a herd."

She grinned. "Is that so? Sounds like you're spending way too much time with Texans, Mr. Appleby. You're starting to talk the way they do."

"We could do worse," Dylan said, returning her grin and putting upsetting suspicions behind him. "The folks I've met here are really nice."

As he watched he saw his wife's smile wane. "I hope you're right. I'm not looking forward to walking into a crowd of unfriendly strangers at the kids' concert."

"They'll be teachers and parents just like us," he countered. "There's nothing to worry about. Besides, as you said, we'll be in a crowd. There's safety in numbers."

Dylan could tell that Grace wasn't convinced. Truth to tell, neither was he. After all, the bullet that had passed through his arm had been fired while they were in a public place. If someone was bent on murder, having a few witnesses standing around was not going to stop them from trying again. And again.

Right now, though, he was less worried about visiting the school than he was about returning to work. He would have to be doubly vigilant from now on. And it didn't hurt to be a little lucky.

That notion stuck in his mind like a thorn until he was forced to admit his error. If there had been divine intervention at work when those cases had fallen, he'd better not make the mistake of crediting a random twist of fate. He knew his wife had been praying for everyone's safety. It was a lot more likely that they'd both been recipients of God's protection because of her prayers than it was that they'd simply escaped injury by chance.

At least that was the way he chose to view the situation. Hopefully, he added, the good Lord would approve.

St. George Elementary School was state-of-the-art and still fairly new, judging by the smaller size of the trees planted on the grounds. Single-story blocks of classrooms were shadowed by an imposing auditorium.

"I've been pulling through the bus lane to let the kids off," Grace told her husband. "I guess it's okay to park anywhere since school's not in session tonight, but I'd rather leave the van on the street if you don't mind walking in."

She noticed that her husband was grinning. "What's so funny?"

"You are," Dylan said as he cruised slowly through the lot. "Why don't you just admit you're ashamed of this old heap and don't want anybody to see us getting out of it?"

"I'm no such thing."

"Oh, really? In that case, how about parking right here?"

Frustrated and a little embarrassed, she fluttered her hands. "Oh, all right. Put it anywhere. It's not as if I plan to try to join the country club."

"You never liked highbrow groups, anyway," Dylan reminded her.

"I liked my new SUV," she countered. "But I guess this beats walking. At least the air conditioner works."

"It had better in this climate." Pulling into an empty slot, he shut off the engine and looked over at her. "Ready?"

"As ready as I'll ever be."

Grace got out and waited while Dylan slid open the side door and helped the children down. To her relief, he hoisted Brandon into his arms and carried him while she herded the other two like a mother hen with her chicks.

"Mrs. Wagner said you're supposed to meet in her classroom," Grace reminded them. "Daddy and I'll walk you over there, then go find a seat in the audience."

"I can go by myself," Kyle insisted.

Dylan was clearly on her side when he said, "Humor your mother. We'll pretend we're not watching if that's what you want, but we're going all the way with you."

Grace smiled at him. "Thanks."

"You're welcome."

It would have been a lot easier for her to deal with her muddled feelings for the man if he hadn't started acting so supportive and understanding. Her unshakable contention that she'd been right about their marriage being over was starting to wane and she didn't like the confusion that had arisen as a result.

Following him as he carried Brandon on his hip and chatted happily with the three-year-old, Grace could envision a different father figure, a man whose priorities had changed for the better, who belonged in their little family as much as she did.

That vision, of course, was totally unrealistic. She knew better. She'd lived twelve years with Dylan, watching him morph into a hardened person whose actions had ended up ruining their lives. He had not put her and his children first then, so why should she believe he would now?

Because he's seen the light? Because his life is in jeopardy and he knows he may soon run out of time to put things right? That conclusion seemed altogether too simplistic.

There had to be more to the improvements she was apparently seeing in Dylan. There simply had to be. Because if he had really repented and turned his life around she knew she'd have to try to forgive him.

God help me, she prayed silently, *I don't want to.*

There was so much raw honesty in that admission Grace was stunned. It shook her to the core to admit she secretly hoped her estranged husband was faking, because if he was, then she could stick to her decision to divorce him.

If he wasn't, however, she was going to be forced to re-think *everything.*

Just when she'd thought she'd had her future figured out, Dylan had done something to shake her resolve.

"Or God did," she mumbled to herself.

That idea was even harder to swallow than her earlier notions regarding her husband!

Entering the auditorium with Brandon, Dylan paused long enough to assess the layout and make a mental note of all the exits, just in case.

As Grace accepted the evening program, a piece of folded blue paper, Dylan directed her by inclining his head and saying, "Let's go over that way. There are plenty of seats and it's right by the side door."

"Is that a good idea?" she asked in a near whisper. "Anybody could pop in."

"And we can also get out in a hurry if we need to," he explained.

"Will the kids be able to see us way back there?"

"You can stand up and wave if you want to, although I imagine Kyle would just as soon remain anonymous."

She smoothed her skirt. "Hey, I'm dressed well and you're not too shabby, yourself, cowboy. I actually like the jeans and boots and that shirt with pearl snaps. It's very…Texas."

"My point exactly."

"Well, don't expect me to go native the way you have. I appreciate the Western culture but I still like my city-slicker clothes." Dylan saw her sober as she added, "I do miss my Italian shoes and Gucci handbags, though. I hope whoever bought them at that sale we told the marshals to conduct before selling the house appreciates their quality."

"At least they brought you your jewelry box. I didn't expect that."

"Neither did I, but I was very relieved. My mother's cameo was in there."

"So were the gifts I'd given you over the years," Dylan reminded her. "I didn't skimp, you know."

"I know. I just wish…"

"That I had shopped in a store like the one where I work instead of an expensive jeweler's?"

"I didn't say that."

"No, but you were thinking it."

He led the way to a group of available folding chairs and took the one closest to the exit he'd already mentioned, positioning himself between Grace and any problems that might come through that door.

Reminiscing, he admitted it had pleased him greatly to be able to buy nice trinkets for her. There had been a time, early in their courtship and marriage, when he hadn't had the funds to spoil her. By the time his finances were in better shape, however, he realized he'd begun using expensive gifts as a way to keep her happy instead of spending quality time with her. That was one of the ways he'd set himself up for the divorce. Yet, at that time, he'd been oblivious to his blunders.

"I'm not sorry I bought you nice things," Dylan said as he relinquished Brandon to her and the toddler turned to sit in her lap. "I just wish I'd realized it wasn't enough."

"The real problem was never the gifts, it was the way you managed to afford them."

Dylan gave a barely noticeable shake of his head and frowned at her. "You didn't know why Munders and Moore gave me those big bonuses when you filed for divorce, so don't go blaming it on my work or the money."

"It's a character trait, not the bonuses," she countered. "You put everything like that first, your job, your loyalty to the firm, your reasons for bending the law to achieve the results your influential clients wanted."

He had no valid argument. "I was wrong."

The surprise on Grace's face was almost enough to make him laugh out loud. Instead he released a wry smile twitching at the corners of his mouth and ended up grinning at her.

As expected, she pulled a face. "Don't look at me like that."

"Like what?"

"Never mind," she blurted, blushing. "Just cut it out."

His drawled reply of, "Yes, ma'am," was meant to amuse her and lighten the tension between them. If he'd had a Stetson he'd have tipped it for added dramatic effect.

Grace stared at him for a few seconds, then gave his uninjured arm a playful smack, hardly touching him yet getting her point across.

His smile broadened. She had just forgiven a little. The way Dylan saw it, the more often they were able to tackle their differences and get past them, the more likely it was that she'd reconsider the divorce and perhaps even stop it from going through.

He assumed the marshal's office could arrange to have their change of residence accepted in any state's court, particularly since they had both signed the original divorce papers, yet he hoped that a tangle of bureaucracy might delay the final decree a little longer. Assuming any of them *had* longer, he added with chagrin.

Eyeing the stage at one end of the auditorium and letting himself systematically assess every figure in sight, he quickly realized Grace had been right. Being trapped among so many strangers could truly turn into a nightmare. No matter how many normal parents and educators were present, there was always the possibility that someone nearby was an assassin.

Dylan was so tense he almost jumped out of his chair when the door beside him creaked and began to slowly ease open.

He swiveled, fists clenched just in case and hoping, if the interloper was after them, he wasn't armed. The past few weeks of manual labor had toughened him up, yes, but bare hands were no defense against an armed attacker.

Dylan paused, waiting, watching, praying.

One end of a tubular metal object poked through the doorway. His breathing stopped. Was that a rifle barrel? Sure looked like one. How was he going to disarm their stalker without endangering Gracie and Brandon, not to mention the rest of the assemblage?

Dylan made a grab for the gun barrel and gave it a yank. To his surprise, there was little resistance!

It took him only a heartbeat to realize he was holding a lightweight plastic toy. The wail coming from the little boy whose prop he had grabbed was the clincher.

Clad like a mountain man, complete with coonskin cap, the child looked to be about Kyle's age, maybe a little younger, and was clearly frightened.

Dylan forced a grin and quickly handed the child back his pretend weapon. "Sorry, son. I guess you just looked too real for a minute there."

Icy, accusatory stares from many of the parents seated

around them led him to add, "National Guard. Overtrained, I guess."

Grace's elbow caught him in the ribs. She mouthed, "Liar," before he could explain further.

"Actually, I did join," Dylan said in an aside. "It was shortly before we had to leave Missouri. I'd seen how much those men were admired and I thought it might convince people that I'd turned over a new leaf."

"People? You mean me, don't you?"

"Last time I looked, you were a person," he quipped, hoping to smooth her ruffled feathers.

She huffed and let her shoulders slump. "What I am is an idiot," she said softly. "I'm actually starting to believe you are trying to change."

ELEVEN

Beth looked so at ease and performed her poetry recital so well, Grace would have been on her feet, applauding, if she hadn't been holding a toddler.

Later, Kyle was part of a chorus that sang patriotic songs in the background while several students acted out the bravery of the defenders of the Alamo, which explained the other child's frontiersman costume.

By the time the scholastic achievement awards had been presented, Brandon had gotten so tired of having to be still he'd cuddled up to his mother and dozed off.

"And that concludes our program. We'd like to invite all of you to stay for refreshments," the principal announced.

Grace was thankful when Dylan relieved her of the sleepy little boy. She would have been happier if Brandon hadn't perspired against her shoulder and left a damp spot, but that couldn't be helped. At least she hadn't worn silk.

That bittersweet thought reminded her that her days of silk blouses and similar luxuries were over, perhaps for good. The up side was the assurance that she was doing all she could to protect her loved ones.

Even Dylan?

Yes. There was no reason to deny that truth, nor did she have the energy to keep battling it out in her mind.

She stifled a yawn. Coming on the heels of his accident at work and her near miss with the speeding car that same afternoon, this evening of mandatory socializing among strangers had worn her to a frazzle.

She strained to see where her children had gone after the curtain closed. "Do you see Beth?" she asked Dylan.

"No, but Kyle's over by the refreshment table stocking up."

"Maybe he has Beth with him. She's so short it's hard to spot her in a crowd like this, even with her red hair."

"Then let's go pick up the one we can see and ask him if he knows where his sister is."

Grace couldn't help sounding anxious. "I hope he kept an eye on her. I forgot to remind him tonight."

"Kyle has his sentry duty assignment down pat," Dylan assured her. "He won't let Beth get too far away."

Threading their way through the milling crowd of adults and excited children, Grace and Dylan worked their way to their eldest son. Kyle had crammed a whole cookie into his mouth so he had trouble answering clearly when his mother asked about his sister.

"Over there," he mumbled, pointing and holding up his hand to help contain flying crumbs. "With a friend."

"Where? Who's her friend?"

Kyle managed to swallow. "Some dorky girl named Jaclyn."

"I see them," Dylan said. "Come on."

Grace was reluctant to meet another unfamiliar person, particularly since she was still having trouble remembering the names of all the teachers and support staff she'd recently encountered. On the other hand, it was a relief to know that Beth was making friends. At least one McIntyre seemed to be adjusting to change.

Dylan led by approaching the slim, dark-haired, well-dressed woman who was speaking with Beth and her pretty little companion. "Hello. I'm John Appleby," he said. "I see your daughter and mine are friends."

"Yes, so it seems." The woman offered her hand and shook his, then turned to Grace. "I'm Miranda Smithfield."

"Mary Grace Appleby," she replied, taking the woman's hand and noticing how soft it was—just as hers used to be before she began doing her own dishes and household chores.

"Pleased to meet you," Miranda said. "The girls have been asking about arranging a playdate. We'd be delighted to have Beth visit."

"Well, I—"

Dylan interrupted. "Sounds great. What did you have in mind?"

"Is tomorrow too soon? We have a pool and I know the girls would love to cool off in it. Does Beth swim?"

"A little," Grace admitted. "She could use some practice, though."

"I'll be sure to keep a close eye on them when they're in the water." The other girl's mother looked down at the eager seven-year-olds. Beth was beaming while dark-haired Jaclyn was so excited she was almost jumping up and down.

"All right. I'll bring her over. Give me your name and number?"

"I have a card," Mrs. Smithfield said, withdrawing a gilded case from her slim leather clutch and handing her card to Grace. "We're in a gated community. If you'll call ahead I'll be sure the guard has your name and vehicle license number so you won't be delayed."

Grace nodded, hoping she wasn't blushing too noticeably. The Smithfields were evidently very well-to-do. That would have been a given, judging by Miranda's posh accessories, even if her neighborhood had not been so exclusive.

And I'm going to show up in that old, beat-up van, Grace thought, realizing almost immediately that she was stereotyping both herself and Miranda. That was wrong on so many levels she simply shook off the unacceptable feelings and broadened her smile.

"Thank you. It sounds like fun for Beth."

"You're welcome to stay for iced tea or lemonade when you bring her," Miranda added. "You and I should get to know each other since our daughters have become such fast friends."

"Well, I…"

Dylan came to Grace's rescue. "Go ahead. I have tomorrow off so I can watch Brandon and Kyle. It'll do you good to get out more."

"Excellent. I'll expect you, then."

Watching Miranda and Jaclyn walk away, Grace caught herself frowning. Unfortunately, Dylan also noticed.

"What's wrong? She seems nice enough."

Grace shot him a grimace. "Nice and rich with perfect hair and nails. She makes me feel like Cinderella."

"Yes, but remember who ended up with the handsome prince in that story," he countered, waggling his dark eyebrows and grinning.

Grace rolled her eyes as she reached for Beth's hand. Dylan had stepped up on her behalf more than once tonight so maybe it wasn't that far-fetched to picture him as a prince, although her first character choice would have been closer to pirate or rogue.

In retrospect, she realized it was his sharp wit and slightly roguish air that had originally attracted her. The trouble was, she had not realized that there was a real outlaw lurking beneath his genteel façade.

If she hadn't been married to him for twelve years and wasn't privy to the criminal actions that had landed them in witness protection, she would be strongly attracted to him, especially now. Her problem wasn't that Dylan lacked appeal. On the contrary, he was not only good-looking, his new incarnation had added a ruggedness that increased his allure. He might not have been born a Texas cowboy but he certainly fit the image well.

And she had an equally strong sense that she did *not* belong there, Grace added with chagrin. That was another aspect of her dilemma. When they'd been dating she hadn't realized that Dylan had come from an impoverished background. In contrast, hers had not been one of great wealth but it had provided a more than comfortable childhood.

Was that why he'd felt compelled to provide so many luxuries? she wondered. Perhaps. But none of that was her fault. Neither was his decision to push the boundaries of the law so far that he'd ended up in serious trouble.

Would it have helped if she had known from the beginning what inner forces were driving him? That was a moot point. Here and now they were simply Mr. and Mrs. Appleby, a struggling young couple with three bright, redheaded children, an old van, a rented duplex and a questionable future.

Truthfully, it spoke well of Miranda Smithfield that she had accepted the family so readily when their clothing was definitely bargain basement.

To Grace's chagrin, it looked as if the wealthy woman was more open-minded than she'd ever be. Fair or not, the conclusion was an indictment against the overly judgmental inclinations she had always been certain she did not possess.

So, what other surprises did the Lord have in store for her? Grace wondered. She cast a sidelong glance at her husband as they shepherded their children out to the van.

Unless she missed her guess, at least some of those surprises were bound to feature a certain lawyer turned roughand-ready Texan and she wasn't sure she was equipped to handle the emotional upheaval she sensed waiting just around the bend.

* * *

It bothered Dylan to let Grace out of his sight, even for an hour or so on Saturday morning, but he also realized she'd been more than compliant thus far. Consequently he'd encouraged her to take her time and visit with Mrs. Smithfield when she delivered Beth to the playdate.

Now, as he paced and watched the clock, he was ruing that decision. Kyle had thrown a tantrum when Dylan had refused to allow him to roam the neighborhood on his own and Brandon was so fussy it was as if the child were the mirror image of his stubborn big brother.

He'd fixed both boys a snack after Grace and Beth had left, then had taken Brandon outside to play catch on the grass in the front yard. Kyle had refused to participate so Dylan had left him alone to sulk.

The three-year-old's skills and coordination were lacking, of course, but he did his best and Dylan found himself laughing at the eager child's efforts.

"'Atta boy! You caught that one."

"I gots it!" The boy kept both pudgy arms wrapped around the large air-filled ball, holding on to it as if it were a shiny trophy.

"Toss it back to Daddy like I showed you."

"No!" Giggling, Brandon took off running. If he hadn't been holding the big ball in front of him he might have stayed on his feet.

Dylan was almost close enough to keep him from being hurt when he fell. Almost, but not quite.

Wild laughter turned to tears.

Dylan gently lifted his youngest son and turned him over so he could brush him off and see if he was really hurt. "You're okay, buddy. It's just a little dirt on your hands and knees."

Brandon remained inconsolable.

"Okay, playtime's over. Let's go back inside, clean you

up and see what your brother's doing, shall we?" He carried the whimpering toddler up the front steps and set him on the porch. "Stay right there while I go get your ball."

The child was still sniffling by the time Dylan rejoined him and took his hand. "Come on. I'd sure like a cookie. How about you?"

"Uh-huh."

"I thought so. First we have to wash your hands." He dropped the inflated rubber ball on a chair in his living room and led the way to the bathroom.

Partway through gently using a wet washcloth on the little boy, it occurred to Dylan that Kyle had not come to see what was going on. That was unusual. Even when his eldest was pouting, he normally checked whenever anyone came or went. That was one of the traits Dylan appreciated.

He held a tissue to Brandon's nose, said, "Blow," and chuckled at his expression of wide-eyed concentration as he complied. "Good boy. You go find Kyle and tell him we'll have cookies if Mama didn't eat them all."

"Okay!" Hurt and humiliation forgotten, Brandon skipped off down the hall toward the bedrooms on that side of the duplex to begin his search.

It warmed Dylan's heart to see how quickly the little boy had recovered. Too bad adults weren't able to switch off sorrow and pain so easily.

He breathed a deep, poignant sigh. It wasn't enough to just pretend that things were all right. Grown-ups might be able to pull off that charade while their hearts were actually still broken. Kids didn't even try to do so until they started to mature and realized it was possible. Maybe that was why Jesus had said believers had to "come as a little child."

Using the unlocked connecting door to Grace's half of the duplex, Dylan was so deep in thought he almost failed to heed a sense of foreboding that suddenly assailed him. He froze to take stock of the apartment, to listen for some telltale clue that he might have overlooked. The doors and windows he could see were closed and the air conditioner was humming. Everything seemed normal.

Nevertheless, he began to make the rounds of each room, getting as far as the hallway when an unusual noise brought him up short. Frowning, he listened carefully. Murmuring? Was someone talking so softly the sound was barely audible?

Or had Kyle come over here to watch TV? he wondered, hoping that was what he was hearing instead of one or more prowlers. Standing perfectly still he strained to hear more, held his breath and noticed his pulse hammering in his temples.

There! There it was again, nearby and high-pitched, like the voice of a woman. Or of a preteen boy. Could Kyle be talking to himself? Perhaps complaining about his parents and how unfair they were? That would certainly be in character.

With several more strides, he reached the center of Grace's small living room and paused again, pivoting to try to pinpoint the sound. Everything was still. Too still. The notion that Kyle might have confronted a prowler and was being held prisoner crossed his mind and he felt a tingle shoot up his spine, an unmistakable threat in the air that reminded him of the internal warning he'd received just before being wounded back in Missouri.

Dylan hesitated, considering his next move with care. If he called out and his enemies had found them, the result could be deadly. If he kept silent, however, his son might be hurt instead of him.

There was only one thing to do. "Kyle?" Dylan said softly, then louder. "Kyle!"

A rustling down the hall was followed by a slamming door and a cynical, "What?"

"Mind your manners," Dylan warned, immensely relieved to see the boy. "Are you alone?"

"Yeah. Why?"

"I was worried something had happened to you, that's
all."

"What could happen to me *here?*" Kyle countered, main-
taining distance as if his father were the real foe.

"Did I hear you talking to somebody?"

"No."

Dylan sighed. Capitulated. "Okay. Never mind. I'm
going to see if your mother has any cookies left and then
Brandon and I are going to share them over at my place.
Want to join us?"

Without comment, the older boy dashed through the
connecting door to the other apartment. Dylan stared after
him, shaking his head and raking his fingers through his
hair. That kid might be as intelligent as they came but he
was sure hard to figure out.

Happily, Dylan located a cellophane-wrapped package
of cookies. When he joined the boys, he found Kyle whispering something to his baby brother. Being an only child,
Dylan had never had siblings to share his deep dark secrets
with, but he could still tell when kids were up to something.

Arching an eyebrow he put the cookies on the kitchen
table and studied his offspring. "What's up, guys?"

"Nothing," Kyle said quickly.

His brother echoed, "Nothin'" and giggled as if privy
to a wonderful confidence.

That was okay with Dylan. He could wait. As long as the
boys were getting along well he was satisfied. In view of
Brandon's age he probably hadn't understood most of whatever his brother had said, anyway. And if he had, he'd be
sure to inadvertently blab sooner or later—probably sooner.

Dylan began to smile, then grin, when he envisioned
the other members of his family and thought, *Too bad Kyle*

*didn't tell Beth or Grace. They'd never be able to keep a
secret for long.*

He chuckled, silently reminding himself he'd better not
express that opinion in front of his wife if he hoped to mend
broken fences and restore their marriage.

As far as he was concerned privately, however, there was
nothing wrong with stereotyping as long as the observa-
tions were patently true.

Take the marshals he'd met, for instance. Every one had
had the demeanor of a law officer, yet each was nevertheless unique. Summers and McCall, the two who had arranged their transfer to Houston, were clearly at odds with
each other over some upsetting incident in their shared
pasts. Trier, who had traveled with them on the plane to
Texas, was different, too. He had a ready smile and an off-
beat sense of humor that actually made him easier to talk
to in tense situations.

Dylan poured and served his children glasses of milk,
then opened the package of cookies before leaving them
and walking to the window to stare out at the empty, ster-
ile backyard and let his mind ramble.

What a pitiful place his sins had delivered them to. How
was he ever going to make things right again?

The negative answer that instantly popped up was unacceptable. There had to be a way to fix this. There simply
had to be. Hadn't he already seen improvement in the way
Grace was treating him?

Or had he? Was he fooling himself because that was
what he yearned for?

He slowly closed his eyes, picturing the past and the
way he and his wife had once loved each other. Did love
like that really die or was it simply laying dormant, waiting for him to carry out his promise to testify and take a
stand against evil?

Although he had strong suspicions regarding the higher-ups in the baby-stealing ring, he had no concrete proof of who else might actually be guilty. Ferreting out those men or women was going to be up to the police and federal marshals. He would do all he could and then step back to wait for the end result, praying that his efforts would be sufficient.

That was going to be the hardest part; wanting to help and not having adequate information to carry the investigation through to its climax.

Would his willing participation be enough to influence Grace on his behalf? he wondered. Or was she simply hanging around for the sake of the kids? He knew concern for their welfare was the reason she'd agreed to relocate. He also knew that she might eventually convince the powers-that-be to place her and the kids separately with more between them than a thin door. That was Dylan's greatest fear.

His family was what gave him a reason for living, for continuing to strive. He could see that clearly now. If he lost Grace and his children, his life would be over just as surely as if his enemies had succeeded in putting a bullet through his heart.

The ringing of his cell phone startled him out of his reverie. He scanned the kitchen counter where he expected to see it and frowned, then followed the noise to the pocket of a denim jacket hanging on a peg by the back door.

Strange. He would have sworn he'd left the little phone lying out so he'd be sure to hear it ring if Grace called. Even if he'd absentmindedly picked it up to keep it with him when he'd gone outside to play with Brandon, surely he'd have slipped it into the pocket of his jeans rather than the jacket. Or would he? The way constant stress had worn him down lately, there was no telling.

"Hello?" was spoken with trepidation.

"It's me, honey," Grace said, instantly allaying his fears. "I thought I should call if I was going to be late. Miranda has invited me to stay for lunch instead of driving all the way home and then having to turn around in a few hours and come back out here. Do you mind?"

Dylan breathed a heavy sigh. "Of course not. Enjoy yourself. We'll be fine, at least until we run out of cookies."

Her soft laugh made him smile as she bid him goodbye.

"That was your mother, boys. She's going to stay with Beth and have lunch so we're on our own. What do you say we order a pizza?"

Brandon cheered and clapped his hands.

All Kyle said was, "Yeah, whatever," before he got up and left the room.

"It'd serve you right if I ordered mushrooms," Dylan called after him. If this was a sample of what was in store for them during Kyle's teens, he could hardly wait.

TWELVE

The Smithfield house was more than impressive, as was everything inside it. From the first step through the front door into the entry with its high ceiling and crystal chandelier, Grace was awed. By the time Miranda had showed her the main floor she was practically speechless.

They made themselves comfortable in the modern metal chairs around a glass-topped table near the pool and watched their daughters splashing and squealing happily.

"So, Beth tells me you haven't lived here long. Where did you come from?" Miranda asked.

"Um, Arizona." This was the worst part of being in witness protection. You had to *lie or die,* as one of the marshals had phrased it. Under the circumstances, Grace figured since God had delivered her into their hands for safekeeping, He wouldn't mind if she followed their rules for survival.

"I've always preferred Texas," Miranda offered with a smile, thereby relieving the pressure on Grace to explain her own pseudo life. "My dad's in politics and my uncle is a judge. How about your family?"

"It's just…John…and me and our three children, two boys and a girl," Grace replied, chagrined to have almost mentioned the wrong first name. That kind of mistake was unacceptable. Above all, she must never relax her guard, never forget who she was supposed to be. And why. *Especially* why.

"That's too bad. My dad doesn't have a lot of time for Jaclyn, of course, but he makes the most of his infrequent visits from Jeff City."

"Jeff?" Grace squeaked.

"Sorry. That's the Missouri nickname for the state capital, Jefferson City. It was named after Thomas Jefferson. There's an impressive statue of him standing at the entrance to the capital building."

"Oh?" Grace had to play dumb or take the chance of revealing why she had blurted out the question. She knew full well what city Miranda was citing. It had been the shock of hearing where the woman's relatives were that had caused Grace's slip of the tongue. The good part about the state capital was that it was located far from St. Louis.

Miranda smiled nostalgically. "I wasn't born until Dad was already in his forties. I think that helps him appreciate my daughter more, too."

"Probably so." Turning to watch the children playing safely in the shallows, Grace didn't elaborate. The less she said, the better, although it was hard to keep from chatting amiably when her hostess was so gracious.

An older woman wearing a starched white apron over a pale blue uniform-like dress appeared on the patio bearing a tray with tall glasses and liquid refreshments. Actual lemon slices floated among the ice cubes in a cut-glass pitcher and drops of condensation were running down its frosty sides.

"Oh, that looks delicious." Grace fanned herself with an open hand. "I am thirsty."

"Then you and I will share this while the girls are swimming. When they get tired we'll dry them off and all have lunch together." She addressed the apron-clad woman. "I'll call you when we're ready for the salads, Louisa."

"Yes, ma'am."

Grace wanted to drink heartily because nervousness had left her parched. Instead she took dainty sips and played the part of a dignified, refined guest.

Which I actually am, she reminded herself. If she'd met Miranda when she'd lived in St. Louis they might have become friends. They certainly would have had a lot more in common then.

And now? Now, Grace couldn't help feeling as if she belonged in the kitchen with the hired help rather than hobnobbing under a canvas umbrella and sipping lemonade.

The spacious patio floor was decorated with bright ceramic tiles set in an intricate mosaic pattern that harmonized with that of the pool. Enormous potted plants, some so exotic Grace had never seen anything like them, were grouped at strategic spots to provide color and appropriate accents.

"You have a lovely home," Grace remarked, meaning it sincerely.

"Thank you. We like it." She was fingering a large diamond ring as she gazed proudly at her suburban domain.

I'll just bet you do, Grace thought, immediately chastising herself for jealousy. Coveting was wrong on so many levels; she was ashamed. This woman was simply being polite and trying to fill the conversational voids with pleasant chatter, rather than sit there mute.

"Let's talk about our girls," Grace suggested, smiling at the two in the pool. "What does Jaclyn like to do for fun, other than swimming?"

"She's taking dressage lessons from an excellent teacher," Miranda said. "You know how young girls love horses. Perhaps Beth can join her sometime."

"We'll see." Grace didn't know how much private horsemanship tutoring cost but she was pretty sure they could never afford it, let alone support an expensive equine—or even rent one from time to time.

"Beth was getting interested in team sports before we moved. I was hoping she'd continue that here, but now that school's about to end for the summer I guess she'll have to wait."

"Children aren't very good at that, are they?"

"They certainly aren't." Grace saw the girls giggling and hanging on to the opposite edge of the pool while they took turns whispering into each other's ears. If it were Kyle she was looking at she'd be concerned that he might be telling family secrets. Beth, she wasn't worried about. The girl was very sensible for a seven-year-old and far easier to reason with than her older brother ever thought of being.

Still, something about the way the children were huddled together gave her pause and spurred her to call, "Beth? Are you and Jaclyn about done? It's almost time to eat and this lemonade is delicious."

"In a sec," the dark-haired girl answered for her guest. Then she cupped her hand around her mouth and renewed their apparently intimate conversation.

Grace was starting to get very nervous. Rather than shout and perhaps reveal her agitation, she rose with a smile, picked up a towel and strolled around the end of the pool until she was standing next to her daughter. "Beth, honey. Come and dry off. It's time to eat."

"But, Mom…"

"You're already getting goose bumps. If you don't want to end up looking like a prune you'd better get out of the water," Grace teased in the hope a lighthearted plea would be more convincing.

She kept pace with the children as they waded to the steps, then wrapped the fluffy bath towel around her daughter's shoulders and began to rub her dry.

Arms folded, the child shivered in spite of the warm air temperature. "Brrr."

"See? I told you it was time to get out."

As Jaclyn ran to her own mother, Grace bent over Beth. "What were you girls talking about just now? It looked like you were telling secrets."

"Uh-uh," the girl said with a shake of her head that sent droplets flying and left polka dots of moisture on Grace's light blue T-shirt.

"Okay, honey. Just remember what Daddy and the marshals told us. We're not supposed to tell anybody who we really are or where we're really from."

"I know."

Judging by the way the child was twisting to get free of the towel, she was done listening. Grace released her to follow Jaclyn and get back into dry clothing before they ate.

She draped the damp towel over the back of a chaise longue next to the pool, then joined Miranda. "Kids."

The other woman laughed delicately. "I know what you mean. They are so imaginative. If I've told Jaclyn once to always tell the truth, I've told her a hundred times, but she keeps inventing wild stories to impress me. I suppose she'll grow up to be a famous novelist. Her creativity is absolutely out of this world."

Wild stories? Grace had to sit before her trembling knees gave out. "Beth is the same way. The tales that girl can tell."

Continuing to grin, Miranda gave her a wink. "So, you and your husband aren't CIA spies on the run from international terrorists?"

"Not hardly." Grace recognized the fear in her weak chuckle, yet persevered. "What other crazy things did Beth say?"

"I didn't catch it all. Jaclyn was babbling something about stolen babies and bad guys. I told you. My daughter has the amazing mind of a fiction writer. It sounds as if both our girls do."

"Right." Grace forced herself to stand again. "I think

I'll go see what's taking them so long. I'd hate to find out Jaclyn was showing Beth your makeup or cologne."

"All right. I'll order lunch brought out and set up while you're gone. We're having chicken salad on a bed of baby greens, fresh fruit cups and sorbet for dessert. Would you like sweet tea, too?"

"The lemonade is fine, thanks." All Grace wanted to do was to get away, far away, yet she knew if she left the Smithfield home too abruptly her hostess might suspect that some of the tall tales the girls had shared were true.

The way she saw it, there was only one thing to do. She'd have to play up the spy story and make it sound so ludicrous that none of the rest was believable, either.

Teeth gritted, she stepped through the French doors and followed the trail of drops and footprints Jaclyn and Beth had left behind on the hardwood floors. Knowing that some poor maid was going to have extra work today made Grace want to pause and dry the floor.

Instead she hurried after her disobedient daughter. If they ended up having to change their names and move again because of Beth's carelessness, that child was going to be sorry.

"We all are," Grace whispered to herself, looking left and right as if she were about to be attacked by invisible enemies. "*I* already am."

Dylan was so relieved to see Grace drive up to the duplex he wanted to race out the door and greet her with a hug. He didn't, of course. That would have been too revealing.

Therefore he waited on the porch with Brandon until Beth and Grace had started toward the house, then let the little boy go.

"Mama!"

"Hi, sweetie." She bent to kiss the top of his head, then

cupped his cheeks and tilted his face. "Looks like some-body had pizza for lunch. Either that or spaghetti."

"Pizza," Brandon shouted. "Daddy made it."

Smiling, Dylan sauntered up to them. "Actually, Daddy had it delivered. How was your lunch?"

"Um, fine."

He wasn't comfortable with her answer or the way she averted her gaze when she spoke. "Grace?"

"We'll talk inside."

"Something went wrong?"

"Probably not. I'm not sure." Passing him she led the way into the house.

By the time Dylan, Brandon and Beth entered, Grace had paused in the center of the living room, obviously wait-ing for something or someone.

Dylan halted. "Do you want to talk to me alone or should the kids listen, too."

"Oh, they need to listen, all right," she said, her tone and somber expression sending a shiver up his spine.

Grace was wringing her hands as she perched on the edge of the sagging sofa. "Beth made a big mistake today and if I hadn't been there to fix things it could have been very, very bad. We might even have had to move again."

Kyle blurted, "No way," before beginning to stare at the toes of his tennis shoes as if they were the most fascinat-ing objects he had ever seen.

Beside Dylan, Beth was looking from one parent to the other, apparently realizing that she was about to be scolded. "I didn't do anything bad."

"Yes, you did," Grace said, being firm but calm. "You told Jaclyn about bad men and stolen babies."

"She didn't!" Dylan was astounded. He hovered over his daughter. "After all the time we took to explain every-thing, how could you have been so foolish? Why, Beth?"

"Ja-Jaclyn kept bragging how important her grandpa was. I just wanted to have something to say."

He felt Grace's light touch on his arm. "It may not be as bad as it sounds. At least I hope not. She also told them that you and I were ex-CIA spies on the run from international terrorists. When I heard about what she'd said, I played up the spy angle and made a joke out of it."

"Do you think it helped?"

"Yes. Mrs. Smithfield seemed to buy the whole exaggeration excuse. I think we're all right. This time, anyway."

Crouching in front of his penitent daughter, Dylan grasped her upper arms. "Look at me. Do you understand what you might have caused by telling that? This is serious, Beth. You must never, never do anything like that again? Do I make myself clear?"

The girl nodded.

Satisfied, Dylan straightened. "That goes for all of you kids. We're not playing a game. You can't go back and start over the way you do when you play on a computer. This is for real. Your mother and I are counting on you to help us make it through."

When he glanced at Grace and saw how pale she was, he dismissed the children, saying, "Go to your rooms. Right now. And stay there to think about what happened and what I just said."

Kyle stalked off, hands in his pockets, his little brother at his heels. Beth ran away sobbing.

As soon as he was certain they were out of earshot, Dylan stepped closer to Grace and opened his arms. Without hesitation she fell into his waiting embrace.

And he held her.

At that moment, in that place, having been faced with a terrible ordeal and coming through as well as she had, all he'd meant to do was to comfort her. To let her know how much he admired her courage.

Still, when he felt her slip her arms around his waist and lay her cheek against his shoulder, his nobler motives went to war with his blissful memories and he began to lightly rub her back through her clothing.

The movement was barely perceptible, yet Dylan felt Grace tense. He stood stock-still, hoping and praying she would not withdraw.

To his relief and delight, she took a deep breath and tightened her hold on him for a brief moment.

Then she leaned back slightly to look up and say, "I'm sorry. I never should have let her go over to the Smithfields'."

Dylan shook his head. "It was as much my fault as it was yours. I'm just thankful you were there to refute what she said about babies and bad men."

"Miranda believed me when I told her it was nothing but a child's tall tale. We actually ended up laughing about the wild stories kids make up to impress each other."

"Then don't worry," Dylan said. "We'll just stay on guard and keep doing the same things we have been. Like the marshal said, if we notice anything odd we'll jot it down and look for patterns."

A poignant sigh made Grace's whole body shudder. Reluctant to release her, Dylan simply stood there and held her close.

At that particular moment he didn't care how long she intended to stay so near. He could not think of a better way to spend the remainder of his day.

Echoing Grace's sigh and matching her mood as best he could, Dylan fought the urge to ask her what else she may have learned while chaperoning Beth. There would be plenty of time for questions later, he assured himself.

Right now, his wife was back in his arms of her own free will. And all he cared about was prolonging the blessing.

THIRTEEN

After her traumatic visit to the Smithfield home, Grace was reluctant to step foot outside the house, even for church the next day. She did realize that children were poor secret-keepers and that she shouldn't blame them too much if they made mistakes. She also knew that the best way to avoid another incident such as the one in the swimming pool was to keep the kids at home as much as possible—at least until they were more settled in their new lives and less likely to revert to their more basic selves.

And how long might that be? Who knew? Certainly not the U.S. marshals.

"I wish Kyle and Beth didn't have to go back to school again," Grace told Dylan at breakfast. She'd been doing her best to avoid mentioning their mutual embrace and figured she'd have a better chance of success if she chose the subjects of conversation.

"There's less than a week left before the summer break," Dylan replied. His gaze traveled to each of his offspring in turn, ending with Kyle.

"So why don't we ditch?" the ten-year-old asked.

Grace answered first. "Because we don't want to do anything out of the ordinary. These people haven't known us for very long and we shouldn't call attention to ourselves. The last thing we need is for some teacher or guidance counselor to start worrying about you kids and show up here to see what happened to you."

"It's only for a few more days," Dylan added. "I think you can tolerate school that long."

"I don't want to go, either," Beth whimpered. "Jaclyn is going to make fun of me because she thinks I'm a liar. I know she is." Her lower lip was quivering. "But I didn't lie."

"I know it's hard to understand right now," Grace said calmly, reaching over to pat the girl's hand. "In order to do the right thing and help the police, your daddy has to hide and stay safe. And we have to help him. Sometimes, the only way to do the right thing is to look at the bigger picture and concentrate on that. The important thing for all of us to remember is that we have to be very careful to keep anybody from figuring out who we are and where we're really from."

"Oh, like some rich kid is gonna care and blab?" Kyle said cynically.

Frowning, Dylan stared him down. "It's not Jaclyn we need to worry about, it's anybody she and her family may know."

"That reminds me," Grace said, wishing she hadn't been so upset when she'd come home that she hadn't remembered to fill him in then. "Miranda says she has close family in Missouri."

"Not St. Louis!"

"No, no. Jeff City. Her father's a politician. And I think she mentioned an uncle, too."

"Did you happen to get their names?"

"Sorry. No. I guess I should have asked but when she mentioned having relatives up there I was speechless."

"Understood. I think you should call her and thank her for hosting you."

"Proper manners probably require a written note since she did invite me to lunch, too," Grace countered.

"You can't ask questions that way and we need to find out exactly who this politician is. Otherwise we won't be able to tell whether or not he's powerful or who his friends in office may be."

"Why does that matter?" Grace asked.

"I don't know that it does." Dylan got himself a coffee refill and held up the pot. "More?"

"No, thanks." Lifting her half-full cup she noticed that her hands were trembling. "I really don't like the idea of phoning Miranda."

"Then bake her a cake or something so you have an excuse to drop by and chat."

Grace rolled her eyes. "Not funny, mister."

He looked confused. "What did I say?"

"You intimated that I can bake when you know I haven't cooked hardly at all in the past ten years." The expression of dismay on his handsome face made her laugh softly. "You didn't think we were paying a cook to just watch me putter around with pots and pans, did you?"

"Well no, but…"

"But because I'm a woman I'm supposed to be great in the kitchen. I get it. Well, surprise, Mr. Appleby. Your wife can't cook worth a plug nickel."

"Is that why we've been having pancakes or cereal for breakfast and ordering takeout for supper? I thought it was just because we liked it."

"We do. I do. Particularly since I don't have a dishwasher." Grace spread her fingers and looked at her hands.

"Then the kids and I will do the dishes for you more often, starting this morning…. Have you decided to go to church?"

"Not by myself. And not today. I'm still quaking in my boots from yesterday's fiasco. I'm not about to take the chance of repeating it in Sunday school."

She paused, then huffed, "But I will phone Miranda

later, after she's had a chance to get home from wherever she worships."

"I don't expect you to learn anything earth-shattering," Dylan told her. "It's just a precaution."

"You mean *another* precaution, don't you? Every time I turn around I'm faced with something else that can go wrong. It's worse than walking a tightrope with no net."

"The marshals are our safety net," Dylan said before casually taking a sip of coffee. "We have to trust them. They know what they're doing."

Looking from her innocent children to her guilty husband, Grace pressed her lips into a thin line and gritted her teeth. Of all her life experiences, this one was the most confounding. She'd been so scared for so long it was beginning to feel normal to keep checking over her shoulder or imagining boogeymen in every closet, behind every door. Was it that way for the marshals? Or were they immune because they could walk away at any time?

Right now she didn't care. All she wanted was a little breathing space, a chance to truly rest and recover some of the strength she'd felt waning. She wanted to be able to step out into the sunshine and raise her face to the Lord's blue sky without wondering if somebody was waiting to take a shot at her. Or at Dylan.

The anger she had harbored toward him was lessening as she watched him interact with their children and experienced feelings of déjà vu that took her back years and years. To a time when life was simple and they were working together to become a healthy, happy family.

Had they ever reached that goal? she wondered absently. She'd thought so before their world was turned upside down. From this vantage point, however, Grace could see that she'd been fooling herself, acting the part of the perfect wife married to the perfect husband with three perfectly wonderful children.

And now? Now, they were probably closer to their true selves than they had ever been. The trouble was, this version of reality also came with built-in, deadly peril.

She was no fool. Whoever wielded enough power to oversee a far-reaching kidnapping and adoption scam without being caught had to have had plenty of help besides men like Dylan. They could not all be white-collar criminals. They had to have muscle behind them. And firepower. And probably even a few law-enforcement insiders, just in case.

Yeah, such as whoever made off with the evidence Dylan had turned in, she concluded. Which meant that even the marshal's office was not secure. They were in charge of keeping others safe, yet they couldn't hold on to a little, pocket-size flash drive for even a few hours. So how secure did that make her and her family?

The honest answer gave Grace the willies. She and Dylan were practically on their own when it came to safeguarding their children and each other. Oh, the authorities could move them around and try to keep their location secret, but in this age of advanced technology, how hard could it be to crack the code and learn everything?

"What is it, Gracie?" Dylan's voice was low, vibrating along her nerves as if a bird's flight feather was slowly being dragged up her arm and down the back of her neck.

"Nothing. I'm fine," she said, hoping he'd accept that.

Instead he moved closer, put his mug on the table to free both hands and held them out to her, palms up.

Grace felt as if she were being drawn to him by invisible bands. Perhaps she was. Perhaps those bands were what had kept them together so far and might eventually pull them back from the brink of divorce.

Although that concept was unnerving, she nevertheless placed her hands in his and boldly met his gaze, saying, "All right. I'm not fine. I'm so scared all the time I'm almost worthless. I don't know what I'd do if I were here alone with the kids."

"But you're not alone," Dylan said quietly, squeezing her hands.

"I could be. First you take a bullet in the arm, then the sky almost falls and crushes you. What else, Dylan? Huh? What else?"

She wanted him to let go of her hands and hug her again but made no move in that direction. His hands were warm, strong and reassuring. That was sufficient for the present moment.

"I don't know, Gracie. We just have to do our best and trust in the marshals."

"And in God," she added, nodding.

"Above all else."

"Do you really mean that?"

She was almost afraid to hear his answer and rejoiced when she did.

"With all my heart and soul," he told her. "I can't explain what happened to me, but somewhere in the midst of all this confusion I surrendered to God and knew without a doubt that He forgave me and He loves me."

Speechless, Grace felt tears welling up in her eyes. To her surprise, Dylan's looked misty, too.

At that moment she knew. God had reached out to Dylan, forgiven him and brought him home.

Her broken heart throbbed. Her mind was spinning. This was the moment she had prayed for. Had dreaded in spite of herself.

Gone were her ready excuses for continuing to hate this man. And in their place was the assurance that it was time to forgive; not in her own strength but in God's.

Staring into his eyes, she licked her dry lips. How much more time might they have? If she put off actually speaking forgiveness and Dylan was killed before she did so, there would be no end to her sorrow.

She took a shaky breath, gathering her thoughts and trying to put them into a semblance of order that would fully express her deepest feelings without giving him false hope. Forgiveness was one thing. Reconciliation was another. They were not mutually exclusive, nor was one a sure sign that the other would naturally follow.

Her lips parted. She started with, "Dylan…"

Instead of listening, he bent and tenderly kissed her.

At the instant their lips met and Dylan realized his wife was kissing him back, he wanted to shout hallelujah. He didn't, of course. Nor did he deepen the kiss for fear of scaring her away.

It was Grace who closed her eyes, slipped her arms around his neck and pulled him closer to increase their intimacy. At that point, Dylan couldn't tell which of them was trembling the most.

Nearly overcome with emotion, he sighed audibly. That was a mistake. It broke the mood and he felt Grace easing away from him so he, too, loosened his hold.

"I'm not going to apologize," Dylan said, stepping back. "You want the truth and you're going to get it. I'm glad I kissed you even if it's the last chance I'll ever have. I still love you, Grace. I always will."

Her fingertips were pressed to her lips. "Don't say that."

He was about to insist that his tender feelings for her were genuine when she explained what she'd actually meant.

"I don't want to think about last chances or running out of time together. It's hard for me to make sense of anything when we're in hiding like this, but I have hope that eventually things will work out between us."

"You mean that?" It was hard for him to temper his elation. "You're willing to try again?"

"I'm willing to consider it," she admitted with a half smile that made her look a little shy, a little silly.

Dylan thought her expression was sweet and charming. There was no way to prevent the grin that split his face, telegraphing his joy as no mere words could.

He gave a nod and blinked rapidly. "That's all I ask, honey. We'll make it. I know we will. Now that I know there's a chance for us I won't let anything spoil it. I promise."

As Grace turned to walk away, a dark specter of doubt arose, gathering force in the back of his mind like roiling storm clouds before a deluge. He might yearn to succeed, to go on living and to resume his role as husband and father, yet he was sensible enough to realize that many aspects of his future were out of his hands. Yes, God had forgiven him. Yes, Grace was starting to come around. And, yes, the U.S. marshals had them in protective custody. Nevertheless, that was no guarantee he would not have to pay dearly for his mistakes, his sins.

Dylan knew from experience that every act had consequences; some good, some bad. He had already suffered the apparent loss of his marriage, so who was to say that he'd be granted the time to experience full healing? At this point he cared less about his prospects for avoiding jail than he did about repairing his broken home.

"Please, Lord, give me more time," he prayed softly. "Or at least show me how to make the most of the days I have left."

Being a realist sure had its drawbacks, he concluded, his mood plummeting even further. He'd had it all, once, and had failed to recognize the fullness of the blessings surrounding him because he was too focused on material gain. Too confused about what was really important.

Success wasn't measured by a man's position in society or his bank balance. It was measured by the people who loved him and whom he loved in return. Those who had prayed for his soul and seen him turn back to God. And those who would mourn when he was gone; who would think of him fondly and miss him greatly.

That was his only lasting legacy. And that was why he so desperately wanted this second chance.

The one aspect that was under his control was his own actions. He'd erred plenty in the past when he'd been relying on human reasoning to carry him through. From now on he was going to count on God.

That resolution renewed his spirit in spite of the reality in which he was trapped. From now on, his prayers would include a plea for divine guidance and the wisdom to recognize God's leading when it appeared. The way Dylan saw it, all he had to do was listen and get out of the way.

"You look like Brandon right after he's made off with the last cookie on the plate," Grace remarked lightly.

Her presence surprised Dylan. "I thought you'd taken the kids over to your side."

"I did. I came back because I heard your cell ringing and wondered why you didn't answer it."

"It rang?"

"Uh-huh." She held it out to him. "It was your boss. Somebody called in sick and he wanted to know if you were interested in some overtime."

Frowning, Dylan palmed the cell phone. "Where was it this time?"

"On the coffee table in the living room."

"Yours or mine?" he asked.

"Yours. Why?"

He was shaking his head. "Just wondered. Either I'm more scatterbrained than I thought or that thing can walk on its own. I could have sworn I left it in the kitchen after you called me from the Smithfields' yesterday. By the way, have you talked to Miranda yet?"

"No. I will. It's still a little early in the day."

Pausing with the cell phone he asked, "Do you mind if I go in to work? I know it's Sunday but I hate to pass up an offer of overtime."

Grace shrugged. "I don't mind. It seems like we've been together more recently than we were in the five or six months before I filed for divorce."

"Not quite. But I do see your point. Okay. I'll call and tell them I'll be there ASAP."

"Ask what time you'll be getting off, later, too."

"Why? Will you miss me?"

Although he kept his query from sounding too serious it meant the world to him to hear his wife reply, "Yes. Something awful."

That was almost enough to keep him home. If he hadn't worried about giving his employer and fellow workers a bad impression of his work ethic, he might have lingered with her in spite of appearances.

Listening to the call go through, Dylan wondered absently if his urge to stay home had been a nudge from his heavenly Father. Was that how God might be guiding him? He didn't think that premise was nearly as likely as the idea that he'd been offered more work because they truly needed the money. After all, it was a blessing to have a job and be able to support his family. Therefore, it was also his duty to do that job to the best of his ability.

"How about my taking the van so you don't have to come get me later?" Dylan asked once he'd firmed up the need to report to work.

"That's fine. Do you have your cell in case I want to contact you?"

He patted his pocket and smiled at her. "Right here. This

time I know exactly where it is." Hesitating, he wondered if she might let him kiss her goodbye.

Finally he settled for a light brush of his lips on her warm cheek and the enjoyable sight of her blush. Redheads were so fair they showed rosy cheeks at the slightest provocation, a trait Dylan had always found endearing.

"Stay safe," he said as he backed away, the key ring jingling as he handled it.

Although Grace nodded and tried to return his smile he could tell she was uneasy about something.

"You sure you don't want to take me to work so you can keep the van?" he asked again.

"No. It's fine. I never liked driving that much, anyway. It'll be nice to have the day off and not have to watch the clock to go pick somebody up on time."

She followed him to the front door and onto the porch.

Dylan frowned when he noticed that he had apparently failed to padlock the door after he'd driven the van. In a hurry to get to work, he shook off feelings of misgivings and opened the garage without help.

"See?" Dylan called back to Grace. "The arm's much better. Almost good as new."

"I'm glad."

She was still waving when he looked back as he drove away, his heart singing regarding their blossoming relationship, his mood so lifted he knew he was beaming.

The stop sign at the corner caused no problems, nor was there any indication that he was being followed. He accelerated smoothly until he reached the traffic light on Richmond Avenue. Applied the brakes. Felt the pedal give.

Puzzled, he pushed harder.

The brakes grabbed, then their effect vanished.

Dylan gripped the wheel. Saw what was ahead in the intersection. Realized he was in trouble.

Panicky, he used the horn for a blast of warning.

One car ahead of him managed to slip around the corner to the right at the last instant, thereby avoiding being hit from behind. A truck crossing in front of him on the green light was not going to be so fortunate.

Bracing himself for the inevitable, Dylan tried his best to swerve but there was no place to go and no way to bring the van to a stop without hitting something.

Metal met. Crumpled. Squealed as it ground together.

The left front corner of the van hit the rear quarter of the passing semitrailer and folded against the truck's steel bumper like a pleated paper fan.

The seat belt held. Dylan pitched forward, wishing the vehicle had come equipped with airbags.

His forehead kissed the top of the steering wheel. Glass shattered. The broken windshield held together but the side windows turned to tiny bits of tinkling crystal that showered him like rain.

Dylan's last thought before passing out was, *Grace is never going to let me drive again.*

FOURTEEN

The sound of sirens in the distance drew Grace to the window. Seeing nothing unusual from inside, she ventured out onto the front porch and stood at the railing so she could scan the neighborhood.

To her left, traffic on the closest side street was beginning to back up. Her concentration was so complete she jumped when a screen door slammed behind her.

It was Kyle. "What's up?"

"I don't know. Probably an accident. It can't be far away because cars are already stopped over there. See?"

"Cool!" He was off the porch, running along the sidewalk, before she could stop him. "Kyle! No!"

Backpedaling, he kept moving away while waving enthusiastically. "I'll be right back."

Grace started down the steps in pursuit, then realized she didn't dare leave the younger children. At that moment, if she had been the type of person to use bad language, she certainly might have done so.

"Beth! Brandon! Get out here," Grace shouted toward the house.

The girl was the first to respond. "Mom? Where are you?"

"Out front. Get Brandon and bring him with you."

Trusting her daughter to follow orders, Grace continued to keep an eye on Kyle. As long as he stayed in sight she'd be okay.

She saw him reach the corner where the line of cars now waited to pass. Several drivers chose to turn off onto their street rather than be stuck in the traffic jam.

Kyle stopped. Turned to peer down the side street, shading his eyes as he did so. Then he faced her, waved his arms as if practicing doing jumping jacks, wheeled around and took off in the direction of the supposed wreck.

Grace wanted to scream. She had never been more angry, or more frightened, in her entire life. They were in a new suburb where she had no close friends and had met only a couple of neighbors. She was on foot. Her kids had separated. And the only way to follow Kyle was if they *all* went.

She could not permit him to get too far away. If he became disoriented and failed to find his way home, she'd never forgive herself.

When Beth arrived with Brandon, the toddler was barefoot so Grace scooped him up and perched him on her hip as she started off. "Kyle just went this way," she explained. "We have to follow him. I want you to stick to me like glue, do you understand?"

Beth nodded soberly. "Why did Kyle leave?"

"I don't know. But when I get him home he is *so* grounded."

Seeing the girl begin to smile about her brother's upcoming punishment helped Grace view the incident in a less dramatic light. "We heard sirens and he went to see what was going on."

"How come you let him?"

Grace grimaced. "I didn't let him. He just took off before I could stop him."

Brandon's pudgy arms tightened around her neck. "Kyle's bad, huh?"

"Yes, honey, Kyle is being very bad."

"I'm a good boy."

Not slowing her pace, Grace kissed his cheek. "That's right. You are. You listen to Mommy, right?"

"Uh-huh. Beth, too."

"Yes." She glanced down at her daughter. "Beth is being good today, too."

After the talking-to we gave her yesterday, she'd better have learned her lesson, Grace added to herself. When Dylan had lectured his brood they had all seemed to take it to heart and for that she was extremely thankful. Although one or the other of them could make an impression on the kids most of the time, a united front with both parents in agreement was most successful.

The fact that Beth had to jog to keep up with Grace's rapid strides didn't slow her down. If she had not had to carry Brandon she might have broken into a run, herself.

They got to the last place Grace had seen Kyle and paused to catch their breath. She didn't spot the boy but she could see that there had been an accident in the major intersection about a block ahead. Judging by the multitude of flashing lights and the throng of traffic piling up, it must have blocked most of the lanes.

What to do now? If she turned and went home there was no telling what mischief Kyle would get himself into. If she proceeded up the block toward the site of the crash, they not only might be in the way, her impressionable children might see something that upset them.

"Hang on tight to my clothes so we don't get separated," Grace told the girl. "I'd hold your hand but I need both arms to carry your little brother."

"Okay. What happened?"

"I don't know. If I tell you to, I want you to close your eyes and not look at it. It might be icky."

"Did somebody get hurt?"

"I think they probably did since I see an ambulance, too.

If it wasn't for Kyle we wouldn't be doing this. It's not a good idea to crowd around an accident and get in the way. Understand?"

"Uh-huh."

Grace could feel a tug on the hem of her T-shirt as Beth followed her instructions, skipping along beside her.

They weren't the only pedestrians headed that direction. By the time Grace got to within a half block of the crash she couldn't tell where the sidewalk ended and the curb began because the area was blanketed with casual observers. Some even held their cell phones over their heads and pointed them in the direction of the wreck to take pictures of whatever was happening out of their line of sight.

The white, metal box of a semitrailer rose above the throng and sat broadside, slightly out of square with the traffic lights that marked the corners. Someone had turned those to flashing red, only, and she could see police officers and firemen rerouting vehicles by swinging lit flares or flashlights.

Beth gave a harder tug. "Eww. What smells?"

"Gasoline. I imagine some spilled." She spoke absently while scanning the milling crowd for the red hair of her naughty son. All she'd need was a glimpse to know it was Kyle. The children's coloring wasn't that common, so they were usually easy to spot, even from a distance.

"Do you see Kyle?" she asked Brandon.

"Nope. I see Daddy."

"Where?" Her heart began to hammer, her knees threatened to give way.

The toddler pointed. "Over there."

That was when Grace noticed the nondescript brown color of a smaller vehicle that was also blocking traffic. Their van! Dylan was here. Was he hurt?

Too shocked to weep, she began to shoulder her way through the gaggle of onlookers that had gathered outside the barrier police and firefighters had established to cordon off the scene.

The first man she reached was dressed in firefighting gear and had his arms outstretched to block her passage.

"That van. It's my husband's. Please, let me through."

He stayed where he was, speaking into a handheld radio to report her arrival and ask permission to let her through the line around the accident scene.

Seconds seemed like hours before he got the official okay, turned back to her and nodded. "You can pass. But watch the glass and debris and be sure you keep those kids with you. They can get hurt running around out here."

"Yes, yes. I will." She dodged past him and made a beeline for the wrecked van, positive that was where Kyle, too, would head, but found it empty. The vehicle had been damaged so badly that it was no longer rectangular and every window was smashed, as if an angry giant had taken a hammer to them.

"Dylan!" Her voice carried over the hum of the crowd and the beeping of a wrecker that was backing up to the rear of the van.

She tried again. "Dylan! Where are you?"

A police officer took her elbow to restrain her. "I'm sorry, ma'am. You can't be out here."

"But my husband…"

"You must be mistaken. There's no Dylan involved."

What had she done! Not only had she left the house when she wasn't supposed to, she'd just shouted a name she was told to never use in public.

"That's his middle name," Grace said while her heart tried to pound its way out of her chest. "He's John Appleby. That has to be his van. He'd left for work a little before I started to hear sirens."

"In that case, come with me."

Although her immediate concern was her husband,

Grace didn't forget her original reason for showing up at the accident scene, either. "I have another son. Kyle. He's ten and has red hair just like these two. Have you seen him?"

"Was he in the car with your husband?"

"No. He was with me. When we came outside to see what was going on, he took off on his own." She swallowed hard. "He must be around here somewhere."

"I'll keep an eye out for him," the officer said. He accompanied Grace and her two youngest to the ambulance where their husband and father was being treated, then excused himself and went back to work.

Although the EMTs had Dylan's head, shoulders and legs strapped to a gurney he managed to reach out to Grace the moment he spied her.

Teary-eyed, she held Brandon aside and bent over her husband's prone figure. "What happened?"

"That's what I'd like to know," Dylan said softly. He crooked a finger to bring her closer. "Call the emergency number for the marshal's office. Tell them what happened and make sure they understand that the brakes failed."

"They *what?*"

She watched him grit his teeth as a medic probed his ribs with a gloved hand.

"When I tried to stop for a red light there were no brakes," he explained. "None. The pedal went clear to the floor."

"They worked fine when I drove it Saturday."

Dylan's eyes narrowed. He took her hand and squeezed before he said, "Exactly. But the garage wasn't locked this morning like it was supposed to be. Make that call."

It was then that Grace realized she had left the house without her purse. "What happened to your cell after the accident? I can use it instead of going all the way home for mine."

"It's in my shirt pocket."

She patted him gently and frowned. "No, it isn't."

"It was. I know I picked it up."

"Maybe it fell out during the crash," Grace said. "I'll go look as soon as I'm sure you're okay."

"I'm fine. This ambulance ride is just a precaution."

"But…you said you didn't want to have any medical records."

"That can't be helped this time."

She gently cradled his cheek while an EMT took his blood pressure again.

"We have doctor's orders to transport," the medic said. "You'll need to step back, ma'am."

"No! I want to go with him."

"We can't take children aboard," he countered. "We're headed for Memorial Hospital. You can join your husband there."

How? Grace wondered, feeling lost and at her wit's end. *I have no transportation and my eldest child is still missing. I'm not leaving here without Kyle.*

Watching Dylan being loaded into the back of the ambulance was tearing her apart, breaking her heart. She blinked away her tears until the doors closed and Dylan could no longer see her. Then she brushed them away before reaching for Beth's hand.

The girl resisted. "Where's Daddy going?"

"To the hospital."

By this time the children were both sniffling. That was almost enough to make Grace break down, too. If it had not been for her annoyance and worry about Kyle she might have given her sorrow free rein.

Thinking that Dylan's missing phone might still be in the van she headed in that direction. A tow truck driver was beginning to winch the damaged vehicle aboard his flatbed truck.

"Wait," she shouted. "I need to look for something inside before you haul it off."

Although the driver did stop the power winch and glance at her, he was not agreeable. "No can do, lady. The cops said nobody is to touch it until they're through." He eyed the two children. "I did catch a kid who looked like those two messing around it."

"When? Did you see where he went?"

The man shrugged. "Nope. I hollered at him and he took off. Sorry." He restarted the winch.

At a loss, Grace fought to maintain self-control. Her body was trembling all the way to its core and she wanted to scream at God for putting her in this untenable situation.

That was when she realized that God had not forsaken her. If anything, He was still looking out for her—for her entire family. Not only had Dylan survived the accident, she and the children had been spared. If she had been driving with her family in the van there was no telling how many of them might have been injured. Or worse.

With her two youngest in tow she began to wend her way through the crowd that was now dispersing. "A little boy with red hair," she announced loudly, "Have any of you seen him? He's ten. Big for his age. Please? Anybody?"

By the tenth time she'd repeated herself she was starting to lose hope. If Kyle had been the boy the wrecker driver had seen, surely he wouldn't have headed home so soon.

"Unless he watched his father leave in the ambulance," she murmured.

Out of options and feeling more unsteady by the minute, Grace began to retrace her steps down Richmond Avenue, praying as she went.

"Please, Jesus. Help us. Help me. Please?"

That was when she spotted him. Kyle was leaning against a fence. One hand held a cell phone. He was pushing its buttons with the other.

"Kyle!" Grace's voice was strident enough to carry over the surrounding din.

The boy jumped as if being electrically shocked. He dropped the cell phone. Stared at his mother openmouthedly.

Grace had to practically drag her daughter to move as fast as she wanted. The moment they reached her eldest she grabbed him by the shoulder and bent, nose to nose. "What did you think you were doing? Why didn't you stop when I called to you?"

"I just—"

"And where did you get that cell phone?"

"It's o-okay," the boy stammered. "It's Dad's."

"Is that what you were doing by the van?"

Kyle's mop of red hair bobbed. "I went looking for Dad. The phone was just lying there in the street, so I picked it up right before some mean guy chased me away."

"What were you doing just now? Who were you calling?"

"Nobody. I just thought—"

"Well, don't think. Don't even move, you hear me?"

Grace released the boy's shoulders and scooped up the phone, praying it still worked.

She pulled up the menu and selected the marshal's programmed number. A man answered.

"This is Mary Grace Appleby in Houston, Texas," she began before he finished introducing himself. "There's been an accident. I need help. Now."

"Where are you?"

"I just told you."

"No," the man said so calmly she wanted to shout at him. "I mean, are you at the house?"

"No. About two blocks away."

"Go straight home, lock the doors and stay put. We'll send someone to you."

"I'll need another car," she blurted, knowing she was coming across as panicky yet unable to stifle her feelings of being in limbo. "And they've taken my husband to the hospital in an ambulance. They wouldn't let me go with him because I had the kids."

"Calm down, Mrs. Appleby. We'll take care of him for you. Just follow my orders and go straight home."

"All right. I will."

"Good. Call me back at this number when you get there."

It occurred to Grace to also tell him that she was so nervous, so in shock from almost losing Dylan—not to mention Kyle—that she could hardly force herself to put one foot in front of the other.

Instead she turned to God, first with more thanks for protecting her and the children, then with a plea for Dylan and finally asking for the strength to make it home on her own.

The quaking that went clear to her bones did not cease. Her heart continued to race and her mouth was so dry she could hardly swallow.

Nevertheless her legs continued to support her somehow and she started back the way she had come.

One step at a time.

One heartfelt prayer after another.

FIFTEEN

The hours Dylan spent languishing in the ER while he waited for the test results were some of the longest of his life. Until the X-rays and scans were analyzed he'd been told he'd have to remain immobilized, just in case his neck or spine was broken. Since he could move his toes and fingers he figured he was fine, but he was educated enough to know he'd better not move before he was given the official okay.

Scrubs-clad nurses and doctors stopped by the curtained cubicle to check him periodically although none of them seemed to know how long he'd have to stay or whether they'd found any serious injuries.

He couldn't see a clock from where he lay, nor did he have a wristwatch or his cell phone, so he lost all track of time except for counting the drips from the saline IV in his arm and watching the level of clear solution in the bag slowly going down.

One of the female nurses he recognized from earlier in the day poked her head through a gap in the curtains, smiled and said, "It shouldn't be long now, Mr. Appleby. I'm going off duty. Don't worry. Somebody else will be checking on you."

"Thanks. I'd like to go home if I can."

"We'll see. Hang in there." She glanced at the monitors

that were recording his vital signs. "Looks good. You're doing fine."

He smiled back at her. "Thanks. Go tell that to the doctor, will you?"

"He'll be in to see you soon, I'm sure." And with that she was gone.

Dylan sighed, noticing as he did so that his right side hurt. Even if he didn't have broken ribs, they were probably bruised from the seat belt.

"At least I didn't fly through the windshield," he murmured to himself, wondering how he might have fared if he had not remembered to use the safety restraints.

The curtain moved as it always did when someone passed and stirred the air. He heard a deep voice ask someone nearby if he was John Appleby and receive a negative answer.

Soft footsteps approached his cubicle. The curtains parted. A burly male nurse stepped through and made eye contact. "You're Appleby, right?"

Dylan would have nodded if his head had not been strapped down. "Yes."

"Glad to hear it."

"Any news on when I can leave?" Dylan asked.

"You'll be out of here soon," the nurse told him before smiling to reveal a cracked front tooth.

Dylan didn't know whether it was the bad dental care, the man's tone of voice or his overall demeanor that made him nervous, but something sure did. The hair on the back of his neck began to prickle and he felt his whole body tensing as the man approached.

The next thing Dylan noticed was that the nurse lacked the customary stethoscope hanging around his neck or sticking out of his pocket. What he did have, however, was a wicked-looking syringe.

"I was told they couldn't give me anything for the pain

until they'd studied the test results," Dylan told him, expecting an explanation or at least an answer.

None came. The man simply held up the hypodermic and removed the safety cap covering the needle.

That was when Dylan realized he was in trouble. It was the nurse's hands that gave him away. They weren't clean. There was dark matter beneath his fingernails and stains on the calloused skin, as if the man was actually an auto mechanic by trade and had come straight from work.

"Stop!" Dylan shouted. "Get away from me!"

With a broadening grin that exposed a dingy row of teeth, the so-called nurse gave a hoarse chuckle. "Hey, man, simmer down." He displayed the syringe. "This is empty. See?"

He pulled back the plunger until the tube was filled with air, then reached for the port on the line to Dylan's IV.

The injected air formed a long, empty space where the liquid had been. Dylan watched the bubble inching its way downward to the needle imbedded in his arm. He wasn't a doctor but he'd read enough mystery novels and watched enough cop shows on TV to know what was about to happen.

There was only one way to stop the air from entering his veins and causing a stroke.

He used his free arm to reach for the tube, meaning to yank it free.

A strong, meaty hand closed around his wrist and stopped him.

Wide-eyed, Dylan watched the bubble slip closer and closer. He was going to die. And there wasn't a thing he could do about it.

Grace made it as far as the steps of her front porch before collapsing. The children gathered around her, clearly empathetic. Even Kyle showed concern.

When he sat next to her and said, "I'm sorry," she slipped her arm around his shoulders and gave him a hug. It was natural for kids to disobey occasionally, trying their wings so to speak. The problem was less about Kyle than it was about the whole situation. And right now she was too spent to waste energy being upset.

"Just don't run off again, honey. Please? I was so worried about you."

"I wasn't gonna go that far, but then I got to thinking about when Dad left and how it might be him, so I had to go see."

"Did you get to talk to him?"

"No. They wouldn't let me."

Grace nodded. "What you did was very dangerous. We smelled spilled gasoline. There could have been a fire."

"There were lots of firemen."

She knew that might not have been enough to keep the boy from being burned but was too weary to argue. Her head was throbbing and her vision kept blurring, not to mention the tremors she couldn't seem to wish away. She felt as if she'd been slogging through hip-deep quicksand instead of walking on a firm sidewalk.

That was exactly how her legs felt, she realized. They were leaden and aching. Each step home had been a struggle to lift her foot and take the next step. And the next. That she had managed to reach the duplex at all was a wonder.

The phone on which she had notified the marshals began to vibrate and sound off in her pocket.

Fumbling it out after three full rings, Grace answered. "Hello?"

"Are you home?" an unfamiliar man's voice asked.

"Who—who is this?"

"U.S. Marshal Colton Phillips, Denver office. I happened to be close by when we heard about your husband's accident so I got the temporary assignment. How is he?"

That query was almost enough to undo Grace. "I don't know. They took him to the hospital. I couldn't go because of the kids."

"Which hospital?"

She racked her brain. "I think the paramedic said Memorial. I didn't get any more details than that."

"It's enough. Since you're home safe I'm not going to stop there first. Once I get backup, one of us will contact you with information and further instructions, if it ends up being necessary. In the meantime, I've asked local law enforcement to keep an eye on your place. They should be there any second."

"Are you going to go find Dylan first?" That had been her most fervent prayer and she was relieved when Marshal Phillips affirmed it.

She wanted to instruct the marshal to tell Dylan that she loved him but quickly thought better of it. If and when she did end up confessing that her feelings toward her husband were changing for the better, she wanted to do it to his face. Wanted to observe his reactions for herself.

And today I almost lost my last chance to tell him, Grace concluded, wondering if she would ever get an opportunity that came at just the right time. Was there such a thing as a perfect time for anything? Or was she going to put off easing Dylan's mind about their pending divorce until it was too late?

That morose thought settled in her core and made her feel as if she were swimming in a pool of regret, about to be sucked under and drowned.

Grace looked to her children and realized she needed to act, for their sakes if not for her own.

"All right," she said, pushing off the wooden steps and getting to her feet. "The marshal said to go inside and lock the doors so that's what we're going to do. March."

She noted that Kyle opened his mouth, probably intending to argue, then apparently thought better of the idea and began to herd his siblings toward the front door.

To her chagrin, she realized that when she had run off in pursuit of the boy she had left her side of the house open. Well, the police who were now pulling up to the curb could check the place for her if it looked as though someone else had been inside.

What mattered most was Dylan. Even if the marshal wasn't at the hospital yet, that didn't mean she couldn't call to ask about her husband's condition.

The phone book listed only one Houston hospital with Memorial in its name, although there were multiple numbers for the various departments.

She chose the Emergency one and began to try to push the appropriate number sequence. Her fingers were quivering so badly she didn't get it right until her third try.

"This is Mrs. Appleby," she said as she clutched the phone so tightly her hands ached. "My husband was in an accident and the paramedics said they were taking him there."

"One moment please."

Grace was about to hang up and try again when the same person returned. "Yes, ma'am. Your husband is with us."

"How is he? When can he come home?"

"I'm sorry. All I know is that he's not ready to be released. But I might be able to let you talk to him."

Grace's heart leaped. "Could I? That's great!"

"Hold please."

Cradling the little phone as if it were Dylan's cheek, she finally let her tears flow freely. If he could talk on the phone, that meant he hadn't taken a turn for the worse after they'd hauled him away.

The nurse returned. "I'm sorry. He didn't pick up."

Grace heard paper shuffling.

"Ah, this explains it. He's being kept immobile. Tell you what. I'll get someone to take him a portable phone and hold it up for him. How does that sound?"

"Wonderful. Thank you so much."

"No problem, dear. I know what it's like to worry about a hubby."

Grace could hear voices overlapping in the background, followed by, "Thanks, Hal. I owe you one."

"An orderly is on his way, Mrs. Appleby. Stay on the line and your husband will be with you in two shakes of a lamb's tail."

The quaint, country expression made Grace smile through silent tears of relief. All she needed was to hear the sound of Dylan's voice again and she'd be okay.

There was a click on the line, followed by a male voice asking, "Which bed?"

"Over there. On the end."

"Okay. Thanks."

If she had been the least apprehensive Grace might not have been so astounded when she heard somebody shout, "Hey! What're you doing?"

The phone apparently hit the floor right after that because there was a sound of plastic cracking. Then a scuffle and banging. Cursing was abruptly cut off.

She screamed "Dylan!" before realizing that there was nobody on the other end of the line anymore, which was just as well since she'd been too overwrought to remember to use his new name this time, too.

In the background she could hear more than one speaker. She sank to her knees on the living room rug and listened as tears streaked her cheeks and dripped onto her T-shirt.

Something was desperately wrong and she couldn't do a thing about it.

Except pray, her weary heart prodded.

Still clutching the phone, Grace called out to God in a wordless plea from her very soul that she hoped reached the heart of her Redeemer.

"The IV!" Dylan shouted.

A younger man, also dressed in hospital scrubs, spun his attacker around, ducked a wild punch and landed one of his own that doubled the assailant over.

There was no time to waste. Reacting as if he knew what he was doing, Dylan yanked the clear plastic tube free of the needle, not totally certain he'd acted in time.

"He put air in my IV," Dylan yelled. "He was trying to kill me."

"Who is he?"

"He doesn't work here?"

"I don't think so."

If Dylan hadn't been strapped down he'd have reacted more assertively. As things stood, the best he could do was a dramatic rolling of his eyes. "Look, just hang on to him and call the cops," he said, almost jumping out of his skin when another stranger abruptly pulled back the curtain.

That man, however, knelt and put handcuffs on the one who had tried to do harm. When he straightened and handed his prisoner off to one of the hospital guards, he told the orderly, "Nice save. Thanks," then turned to focus on Dylan. "Marshal Colton Phillips. I understand you've been having some problems."

Dylan huffed. "You might say that. This is the second attempt on my life. The third if you count last week."

"Last week? I didn't see anything about that in your file."

"You should have. I called it in."

"Okay. I'll check again when I have time. Right now we need to concentrate on how you landed here."

"Where did you say you were from?" Dylan asked cautiously.

"I'm based in Denver."

Then what are you doing in Houston? And how do I know I can trust you? "Mind if I see some ID? It's been that kind of a day."

The light-haired, blue-eyed marshal took out his badge wallet and flipped it open to reveal his full credentials. "Does this make you feel better?"

"Some. I wonder if I'll ever feel normal again."

"Hopefully. The police who responded to your accident tell me you kept insisting that someone had tampered with the brakes on your van. Have you been keeping the garage locked?"

"Usually," Dylan said. "It didn't seem as necessary during the day when we were at home and I guess I forgot to check last night. That door's too heavy for my wife to handle by herself and when my arm was still real sore I had trouble with it, too."

"I'll make a note of that and get the problem corrected." Phillips said. "What else can you tell me?"

"Not a whole lot. It's been quiet except for the freak accident at the warehouse store where I work."

"Accident? When?"

"A week or so ago. That's what I meant when I told you I'd called. Marshal Trier, the same guy who escorted us to Texas, took my report. He said not to worry unless something more happened." Dylan pulled a face. "Does landing in the hospital and having some lowlife come after me here, too, count?"

"I'd say so." Phillips was apparently paging through digital files on his palm-size phone. "I don't seem to see that particular report."

"Well, I made one. And I told that same marshal about a motorcyclist who tried to run me down when we first got to Houston."

"Were you sure the biker was after you?"

"No." Dylan shrugged as best he could while still strapped down. "But it sure seemed like it at the time."

The appearance of a doctor and two regular nurses caused the marshal to step to one side.

"Are you going to spring me?" Dylan asked the doctor.

"That's the plan. I'll make an appointment for you with a neurologist, just in case. Feel free to cancel it if you don't have any more symptoms, like headaches or dizziness." He shined a penlight into Dylan's eyes, making them water. "Looks good to me. I'll sign you out. Do you have a ride home?"

"I'll take him," Phillips said flatly. He was concentrating on the information on his phone and watching the lobby at the same time. "My backup just got here. They can take care of the prisoner for me and explain everything to the police."

The physician arched an eyebrow. "Police?"

"It's a long story," Dylan told him with a sigh and a visible wince.

"Your ribs may bother you for a while," the doctor said. "Don't worry. Nothing's broken. I wouldn't do any diving off a high board for a while. Stuff like that. Otherwise, you should do well."

"Thanks, Doc." He let the nurses help him raise his upper body, then swung his legs over the side of the gurney until he was sitting on the edge of it.

"Has somebody checked on my wife and kids? Grace must be frantic," Dylan said as soon as he caught his breath well enough to speak through the pain.

"They're at home and the local police are keeping an eye on them for us. You can use my phone to call from here if you want. I'll take you to them as soon as you're checked out. How do you really feel?"

Dylan made a face and looked the man straight in the eyes as he said, "Vulnerable."

SIXTEEN

Frantic, Grace had kept the line to the hospital open until it had gone dead. Then she had paced and fretted until Dylan had called to reassure her. She did appreciate the effort, even though her jangled nerves insisted she'd have to see him in person before she'd totally believe he was okay.

The kids spotted their daddy arriving home before Grace did. Squealing with delight, all three barreled out the front door and dashed up to him while she stood back, assessing the man who had escorted Dylan. There was no doubt another marshal had brought him. The familiar demeanor and dress code said it all. So did the fact that her police watchdog was leaving.

When Dylan's gaze met hers and he began to smile, she was nearly overcome. The most amazing facet of their current relationship was how vitally important he had become to her. Whenever they were apart she yearned to be reunited, and when they were, she could not get enough of him. She might have likened it to their first love if a much deeper sentiment had not been involved. His presence both calmed and elated her, giving her the feeling that their hearts and minds had always been joined.

Descending the porch stairs, Grace approached Dylan, then paused while he continued to greet the children. When he straightened and took a step toward her she realized that nothing in the universe could stop her from falling into his arms and embracing him.

Dylan accepted the show of affection without hesitation. As he held her close he whispered, "It's okay, Gracie. I'm fine."

Although she had to force the words she managed to admit, "I'm not. I was so…so afraid." Her breath shuddered. "When I heard the phone hit the floor and you yelled in the background, I thought my heart was going to burst."

He was gently rubbing his wife's back, murmuring to her, when the marshal broke the mood. "Time to go inside, folks. We're sitting ducks out here."

Dylan loosened his hold on her and gestured. "Sorry. Grace, meet Marshal Colton Phillips, from Denver."

"Denver?" She made a face. "Whatever. It can't be any stranger than the other things that have been happening around here."

"We need to discuss all that," Dylan said. "In the house where it's safe."

Grace quickly reverted to her role as a parent and shooed her brood toward the front door. Dylan and the marshal followed.

Once the door was closed and locked, she felt like a party balloon with a pinhole leak, slowly and inexorably deflating. If she had ever been this weary, this totally spent before, she didn't know when. Even during the birth of her children, which had been a physical challenge of course, she hadn't been nearly this emotionally drained.

"Can I get anybody some iced tea? Coffee? Lemonade?"

Both men politely declined while the children began to clamor for a snack.

"If you two will excuse me, I'll take the kids over to the other side of the house and feed them there so we can talk. Be back in a minute."

The last thing she intended was for the children to listen while Dylan and the marshal discussed what had happened, both at the accident scene and at the hospital. What little her husband had told her when he'd finally phoned to explain the latest attempt on his life was plenty.

Obviously someone had discovered where they were hiding. That was a given. Two questions were critical. How had their cover been blown and what could they possibly do to keep it from happening again, no matter where they were sent?

Mulling it over caused Grace to recall her failure to contact Miranda Smithfield, as promised. While she was cutting up an apple and washing grapes for her kids she made up her mind to follow through with that vow, even if it was now a moot point. She didn't believe for one second that the wealthy woman would have connections to criminals who might care about a family in witness protection, yet asking who the politicians in her family were could rule them out. That was important, too.

As soon as she rejoined the men in Dylan's side of the duplex she mentioned her plan.

"We could have taken care of that for you if you'd asked," Marshal Phillips told her. "It would have been smart to clear the family with us, anyway." He huffed. "Since you've already made contact, I supposed you may as well give the woman a call and find out the easy way."

Settling herself on the sofa while the men relaxed in armchairs and conversed quietly, Grace got out the number and placed the call.

She began to smile when Miranda answered politely.

"Hello! This is Mary Grace Appleby. I'm just calling to thank you again for your hospitality."

"Not at all."

Grace immediately sensed something off-putting about the other woman's tone. It was almost as if she'd flipped a switch and turned coldly unfriendly as soon as Grace had identified herself.

"Well, Beth and I had a lovely time."

"That's nice."

Okay. It was official. Miranda was *not* happy to hear from her. What had changed? They had seemed to be getting along splendidly twenty-four hours ago. Had the well-to-do woman simply decided to stop slumming? Or could her change of heart be due to the wildly imaginative stories the girls had exchanged?

At this point, Grace didn't see how she was going to bring up the subject of Miranda's Missouri relatives without sounding too nosy so she held back. One look at Dylan's and the marshal's expression told her they had picked up on her confusion.

"Well, I won't bother you further. I just wanted to express my thanks."

It was not a big surprise when Miranda hung up abruptly.

"Whew! That was strange." Frowning, Grace gazed at her husband while the marshal began speaking on his own cell. "Until just now I'd thought she and I might become friends."

Colton Phillips had risen and paced across the room. When he ended his phone call, he faced the couple. Grace could tell he was not happy. Well, that made three of them.

"Miranda Smithfield's maiden name was Simms," he announced, staring straight at Dylan.

Grace saw color draining from her husband's face.

"Simms?" Dylan's jaw dropped. "Is her father a judge?"

Phillips shook his head. "No. Her dad is Congressman Peter Simms. Her uncle Simon is the Judge Simms you've dealt with."

Grace gasped and covered her mouth. "You *know* him?"

"Unfortunately." Dylan was slowly nodding. "If Miranda happened to mention our three red-haired children and what Beth said about stolen babies, it would have been fairly easy for somebody back in Missouri to figure out who we were."

"And to send an assassin after you," the marshal said flatly. He turned his back and made another call.

Grace's gaze met Dylan's. "Do you really think that's how they found us?"

"It has to be. Judge Simms was the one who signed off on the shaky adoptions I handled. I'd thought he was just another gullible do-gooder, like me, but I may have been mistaken."

"What about the congressman? Do you think he's involved?"

"I strongly doubt he'd take a chance like that and jeopardize his political career. Of course, he may have simply mentioned it to his brother and the judge told somebody else, and so on. Their family connections to Beth's little friend aren't proof of criminal intent."

"Spoken like a lawyer," Grace said dryly. "Off the record, counselor, what do you think?"

Dylan's brow furrowed as he cast a furtive glance at the marshal. "Personally? I think we'd better start packing."

"I have orders to return to Denver ASAP. There will be a black-and-white on the street until Summers and Mc-Call get here. They're on their way," Marshall Phillips announced. "They've been talking to my old boss, Hunter Davis, and they'll have a few new questions for you when they get here."

"They're coming to Houston?" Dylan asked. "What about the Missouri connection we just discovered? Who's going to look into that?"

"Rest assured that somebody will. We're trying to coordinate our efforts to avoid wasting time by duplicating tasks. One of the reasons the office here in Texas was so willing to send me to assist you is that I was involved with the FBI in locating one of the stolen babies."

"That case is tied to those adoptions I handled, too?" Dylan felt as if there was a three-hundred-pound boulder lying in his stomach. "Unbelievable." He raked his fingers through his hair. "I wish I had my old files. They were filled with pictures of those poor kids."

"Without doing an age-progression, they'd probably be too vague for an ID by now, anyway." The marshal poked at his cell phone, then held it out to display the image of a blond toddler. "Here's a picture of the baby I helped rescue. Cute little thing, isn't she?"

"Yes." Dylan answered out of politeness, barely glancing at the picture. If only he had questioned more, had listened to his conscience when it kept insisting that something about his assignments was terribly wide of the mark.

Part of the problem was that his choice of the law as a career had been made for the wrong reasons. He could see that now. He'd been chasing prestige and a high salary when he should have been seeking fulfillment and contentment.

Would a younger Grace have even looked at him twice if he had not had grandiose plans for his future? Probably not. However, she was no longer the same person she'd been back then and neither was he. They might legally be husband and wife but they were very different people than they had been twelve years ago.

Recognizing that, Dylan came to the conclusion that it was not going to be enough to merely try to renew their former relationship. They were going to have to get to know each other much better, to perhaps eventually fall in love again, assuming they were still suited to each other. God willing, they would be, because he could not imagine any life without her—and his children.

* * *

Choosing what to pack was much easier this time. Grace figured she could cram everything important into the suitcase she'd arrived with, except for a couple pairs of cheap sandals she'd bought to wear in the warmer weather of the Texas gulf coast. They'd already had daytime temperatures near ninety, and it was only May. No telling how hot the summer would be.

That notion made her smile wryly. It no longer mattered to her how hot it got in Houston. She wasn't going to be there long enough to suffer in the heat. The thing that did surprise her was her willingness to pack up and move on. It seemed as if the first move had loosened the ties to her former home and other material possessions, leaving her freer to follow whatever path the Lord set for her and her family. They were the truly important things, not the stuff hanging in their closets or the money in the bank accounts.

Beth entered the bedroom, saw Grace pulling clothing off hangers and ran wailing down the hall to tell her brothers. Kyle was the first of the children to return and confront his mother.

"What are you doing?"

"Packing," Grace said calmly. "We're going to have to move again. We have no choice. If you want to help, you can find your brother's backpack and start filling it for him."

"Are we going home?"

"This is our home now. At least it was. I doubt we'll ever go back to St. Louis, if that's what you mean."

"Well, *I* will."

Before Grace could reply, the boy had wheeled and stomped off, leaving his siblings standing in the doorway. Beth was crying. Brandon looked more confused than upset.

"Beth, honey, go fetch your daddy for me, will you? Tell him I need his help with something. Okay?"

The child sniffed, nodded and disappeared.

"Brandon, how about you go pick out your favorite toy? That's a good boy. And don't let Kyle bug you. He's mad at me, not at you."

She was alone and chewing on her lower lip when Dylan appeared.

"What's up?" He eyed the messy piles on the bed. "You packing already?"

"Better me than the marshals," she countered. "It's Kyle I'm worried about. He's having a hissy fit over this new move. I think you should go talk to him. I tried to explain but he wasn't in the mood to listen."

Dylan heaved a long sigh. "Not surprising. I'm all grown-up and it's not to my liking, either. I can't imagine how disastrous this situation feels to him, particularly since we haven't shared much background information."

"Oh, I don't know. Kids pick up a lot more than we think they do. Look at Beth."

"True." He shoved his hands into the pockets of his jeans. "Okay. I'll go talk to him. Which way was he headed?"

"To his room. Should I come along?"

"No. I'll give a shout if he hog-ties me and stuffs me in the closet," Dylan quipped. "Otherwise, I think I can handle one grouchy ten-year-old."

Grace was still smiling when he turned away and started down the hall. No matter how dire a circumstance was, Dylan always seemed able to find the lighthearted side of it, even if he had to make up something crazy, the way he had just now. That was one of the things she loved about him. One of *many* things, she reminded herself.

In the distance she heard him calling "Kyle" over and over. Finally he returned to her room.

Grace stood stock-still, staring at the distress on her husband's face. "You didn't find him?"

"No." His brow knit. "He could be hiding. We'd better both look."

Heart pounding, she threw aside the blouse she'd been folding and went with Dylan. "The other kids can help. They're more likely to find him than we are since it's us he's upset with."

"Right."

Mustering their forces, such as they were, Grace and Dylan assigned the two younger children to poking through closets and small hiding places while the parents ventured into the yard.

"We don't want to yell too much and alert the neighbors," Dylan cautioned. "If we don't locate him soon I'll call the marshals and they can bring in the local police again if they think it's necessary."

She clamped a trembling hand around his wrist. "I think it's necessary *now*."

"Maybe he just took off like he did this morning. It's certainly possible."

"He wouldn't dare do that again." The moment the statement was out of her mouth, Grace realized she was wrong. If Kyle did it once, he'd do it twice. Besides, she'd been so concerned about Dylan's possible injuries she'd failed to discipline the boy adequately, either at the accident scene or later, at home. It was no wonder Kyle didn't respect her when she was so lax about holding him responsible for his misbehavior.

Circling left while Dylan went right, they met at the rear of the property and entered the fenced yard.

Grace didn't try to mask her worry. Looking at her husband she could tell he shared those angst-ridden sentiments. "What now?"

"We search the garage, just in case, then go back inside."

"To call the marshals?"

He was grimacing as he nodded and said, "Yes. It looks like we could use their expertise."

Something inside Grace insisted she try to think of ways to make their situation bearable, if not for Dylan, for herself. "I'm sure this isn't the first time a child has run away from protective custody," she offered. "Do you think Kyle was actually mad enough to take off?"

"I hope so," Dylan said soberly.

"You *hope* so? Why?"

"Because if he did leave on his own, that means he's still relatively safe. If he didn't…"

That unfinished sentence gave Grace the shivers all the way to the marrow of her bones. It seemed crazy to wish their ten-year-old had run away from home, yet she had to agree with Dylan. Kyle *must* have left in a huff.

The alternative was simply too horrible to consider.

SEVENTEEN

"Okay," Dylan said. "While I call the authorities, you go find the other kids and corral them, just in case. I'll start with Marshal McCall since he's the guy Colton Phillips talked to earlier."

Watching his wife's shoulders droop gave Dylan a jolt. If the indomitable Grace McIntyre was that disheartened over their son's disappearance, she must be far more frantic than she was letting on. He could identify with that. The moment he'd heard that Kyle was missing he'd had a hollow feeling the size of a Smart Car in the pit of his stomach.

He pulled out his cell, reported that they were unable to locate Kyle and was instructed to stay in the house and wait. Their relocation team was on its way and local authorities had been alerted to keep an eye out for the missing boy as they cruised the neighborhood.

Dylan had just ended that call when the phone vibrated, startling him so much he almost dropped it. Had the marshals forgotten to tell him something?

"Hello?" he began before his hopes were dashed.

"Nice to hear your voice again."

"Who is this?" Dylan demanded.

"Never you mind, buddy. We just wanted to make sure you figured out what was going on. It'd be real sad if something happened to the kids."

"What kids? You must have the wrong number."

The caller laughed hoarsely. "Oh, we've got your number, all right, in more ways than one. It's too bad we had to go to plan B."

"I have no idea what you're talking about." Dylan figured stalling and denial were his best options. When Grace returned with the other cell phone, he would signal her and she could contact the authorities ASAP while he kept this caller busy.

The man's next expression began as a laugh and ended sounding more like an animal's growl. "The crash, you fool. Did you think it was an accident?"

At this point, Dylan was tempted to insist the guy had the wrong party and hang up. He didn't. The more he could get this person to admit, the more information he'd have for McCall or whoever he sent in his place.

"You were there this morning? Are you a reporter?"

"You really are dense, man. Yeah, I was there. I was in your garage to fix your car the night before, too. That padlock is a real joke. So, how'd you like your brake job?"

"I've had better." Anger was beginning to boil to the surface and Dylan didn't fight it. This lowlife had tried to injure him and could easily have wiped out his entire family. Nobody was going to get away with that if he could help it.

"Yeah, well, I aim to please." The thug chuckled. "You did give us a run for our money, McIntyre. If it hadn't been for those dumb kids of yours we might still be looking for you."

So, that *was* how they'd been found. "What do my kids have to do with this?"

"Plenty. For starters, your girl talks too much."

"Simms? This goes back to him?"

"Not so fast," the gruff caller said. "It was your boy who started the ball rolling. Guess he was lonesome. He called a couple of his friends in St. Louis. After that, we had you cold."

"Kyle used the *phone?*" Suddenly those times when his cell had ended up in strange places were starting to make sense. So was the rundown battery in Grace's unit. The boy had apparently availed himself of whichever telephone he could lay his hands on, then had returned it without being caught. No wonder he'd been acting so strangely. He not only had a chip on his shoulder, he had a guilty conscience.

"Yeah," the man said. "He's quite a little communicator."

Dylan was gritting his teeth. At this juncture there was no use denying who they were or where they lived. Their enemies seemed to have everything figured out. The only puzzlement was this phone call. Why would an assassin bother to warn them?

"What do you want?"

"I'm the one who should be asking you that question." Another wry chuckle. "Seen your oldest kid lately?"

Icy fingers of fear crept up Dylan's spine and nearly strangled him. "What are you talking about?"

"I think you know. It was actually easy. We caught him climbing out his bedroom window."

Dylan's jaw went slack. At the periphery of his vision he sensed movement. His head snapped around. It was Grace. And the other children. How long had they been standing there? How much had they overheard? Judging by their stricken expressions, plenty.

"Tell me what you want. I don't have much money, but…"

"Oh, puh-leeze. We're after something much more important. Your silence. It's simple. If you testify, the kid dies." He snapped his fingers. "Just like that."

"Wait! Let's talk about this."

"Why? It's not open to discussion."

Dylan's mind was spinning. There had to be something better to offer for Kyle's freedom than mere money. Even if he'd still had access to the assets he'd once treasured they probably wouldn't be enough to ransom his son.

His heart and mind called out to God. In moments, peace and calm flowed over him. He was assured of what course to take. Now, all he had to do was convince Kyle's kidnappers to accept his plan.

"I have a better idea," Dylan said, fighting to keep any hint of nervousness out of his voice. "Instead of babysitting him for months while we wait for the trial, why not trade him for me? That way you'll be positive I won't talk."

"Oh, sure, and you'll have the cops waiting to grab us when we show up for the exchange."

"I won't, I swear. I'll do anything you say, meet anytime, any place you tell me to. Just let my son go."

After a heavy silence, the caller said, "We'll think about it. Stay close to the phone. I'll call you back if we decide to take your offer. And no cops. Understand? They show up, the kid dies."

"I understand." Dylan was so shaken and so relieved he almost blurted an undeserved, "Thank you."

Grace didn't have to hear both sides of her husband's conversation to get the gist of it. The agony in his eyes told her more than enough, and when he began to negotiate to trade himself for their son she felt faint.

Blinking away the flashing, colored lights on the fringes of her vision and taking deep, shaky breaths, she managed to hang on to her equilibrium long enough to reach Dylan's side. "Tell me," she demanded. The children were holding on to his knees and he laid a hand atop each of their heads in turn, ruffling their hair. "Not here. Not now."

Grace bit her lower lip and waited for him to elaborate. When he did not, she demanded, "Yes. I want the whole story."

She watched her husband take a faltering breath before he said, "They have Kyle."

"You believe it?"

"Yes, I do."

"Did you recognize the caller's voice?"

"No. Come on. I need to check something in the boys' bedroom."

Because he grabbed her hand and tugged, she stayed with him, although her shock and anger were almost enough to make her jerk away from his touch. This crisis definitely called for sticking together but that didn't mean she was ready to stop blaming Dylan. For everything.

One glance behind told Grace the other two children were following. She gritted her teeth and bit back the sobs that were almost choking off her oxygen. If what she thought she'd overheard Dylan saying to the thug on the phone was true, she might be close to losing almost half of her little family.

It wasn't fair. None of this was. Grace was about to say so when they came to the closed door to the boys' room. Dylan gave it a push.

She felt his grip on her fingers tighten and peered past him. "What is it? I don't see anything wrong."

"The window," he said, keeping his response low. "They said they caught him climbing out this window. Look. It's wide open and the screen is missing."

It was all she could do to stay on her feet, let alone speak intelligibly. "They really have him?"

The fact that her husband was silently nodding didn't make nearly as big an impact on her fragile emotional condition as something else about him did. There were unshed tears glistening in his eyes.

If Dylan had been able to make his unknown enemies contact him again by the sheer power of his will, they already would have. Grace had always been the one in their family who lacked patience but his anxiety now rivaled hers—and she was a ticking time bomb.

Pacing, he kept scowling at his cell phone and checking the time.

"It's not going to ring any faster if you walk the floor with it." Grace kept clasping and unclasping her hands."

"I can't sit still."

"Then come with me while I pack for the kids so I have something to do, too."

"You don't need my help with that."

"All right," she said haltingly. "Let me put it this way. I don't want to be alone right now. Satisfied?"

"Completely."

Crossing the small living room, he followed her through the door to the other side of the duplex. Could she have meant she actually wanted to keep him close, or was he imagining more personal interest because that was what he yearned for? It really didn't matter at this point. What did count was getting their son back.

Dylan had recognized that there was only one way to accomplish that and had offered himself in Kyle's place because it was necessary. He knew what he was doing, he simply wasn't convinced that Grace would let him go. The marshals certainly wouldn't allow it if they knew what he'd planned, which reminded him of another problem.

"I need to call McCall back and tell him Kyle is staying at a friend's house so he cancels the search and doesn't show up here himself."

She had reached for a tissue and was blotting her tears. "Hold on a second. Aren't you going to let him help capture the kidnappers?"

"No," Dylan said flatly. "After you get Kyle back, you can inform the marshals about what I've done. But not a peep until the boy is safe and sound."

"That's crazy." Grace was nearly shrieking at him.

"Only if something goes wrong."

She rolled her eyes and threw her hands in the air. Rivers of tears were streaming down her pale cheeks once again and her eyes were puffy. "What can possibly go wrong? My son has been kidnapped. My husband is planning to trust some crooks he doesn't know. And a bunch of people connected to the baby-stealing ring were murdered in jail." She sniffled, gulping back noisy sobs. "Where did you get your brains? In a box of breakfast cereal?"

He knew there was no way he'd be able to convince her that his way was best, particularly when she was so hysterical, yet he continued to believe they had no other choice.

She finally pulled herself together enough to ask, "What do we do if they don't accept your offer?"

"Then we contact McCall or one of the other marshals, I guess." Dylan raked his fingers through his hair as was his habit when thinking. "I don't want you anywhere near me when we make the trade."

"I am *not* letting you do this alone. Kyle is my son, too."

"Think for a second. We have no safe place to leave Beth and Brandon and we don't want them involved. It's too dangerous." He pressed his lips into a thin line of determination. "It's bad enough that Kyle has to be there."

"Who's going to take charge of him when the criminals take you away? Huh? Have you thought of that?"

"No." Dylan heaved a noisy sigh. "One catastrophe at a time, Gracie. They haven't even called back yet."

"You still think they will, don't you?"

"It's the smartest thing they can do. My hope is that their boss, whoever he is, didn't get his brains out of a cereal box the way I got mine."

"I shouldn't have said that." When she laid her hand on his arm, her fingers were trembling. "I'm just so scared."

"We're all in God's hands," Dylan reminded her. "I do

believe God is on the side of good. It's just that I also know He may have other plans than what we'd prefer."

"Amen."

Opening his arms, Dylan offered an embrace and was relieved when his wife accepted it in spite of her off-putting agitation and righteous anger.

Each time they touched, no matter how innocently, he and Grace seemed to grow closer, more emotionally and spiritually connected. Truth to tell, he imagined that they were more "one" at that moment than they had been in the days of their supposedly ideal marriage.

As Grace laid her cheek on his chest and he placed a kiss on her silky red hair, Dylan silently thanked his heavenly Father.

Unexpected warmth swirled around them, as tangible as if God were wrapping them in a blanket of His peace and divine, everlasting love.

That was the moment when Dylan realized they might very well be receiving this experience as a special gift. A beautiful, lasting memory that he could call upon to sustain him in the coming trials and that Grace could cling to for solace if and when he was taken from her.

As sobering as that thought was, he nevertheless gave thanks. Many men never had the chance to make peace with those they had wronged and he had already accomplished that much. To hold his wife like this, to know how much he cared for her and to impart that love in a physical and spiritual way was a lot more than he deserved. A lot more than he had hoped for when he'd been praying for the restoration of his broken marriage.

Dylan tightened his hold, unmindful of the pain in his bruised ribs, and felt her answering squeeze. He desperately wanted to confess his renewed devotion, yet he feared Grace was not in the right state of mind to hear and accept it.

Then again, if she did share that same sense of deep, abiding love, his declaration might cause her to behave in a way that was not in her best interests.

He had to handle the exchange of prisoners on his own. Without Grace's help. It was the only way he could be assured she'd remain safe. The only way he saw to preserve what was left of the family he had nearly thrown away because of greed and a misguided sense of right and wrong.

The guilt was his and his alone. He would face the consequences the same way. Alone—except for Jesus Christ.

Just as Dylan was entertaining that very thought, his cell phone rang and he released Grace to answer it.

"Yes?"

"We're ready to trade."

Dylan nodded as he said, "Agreed."

The plan was in motion.

There was no turning back now.

EIGHTEEN

If Grace hadn't cared what happened to her husband and innocent son she might have let Dylan handle things his way. It was the concept of losing them both that spurred her to act.

Once Dylan had confided the details of his upcoming rendezvous with Kyle and the kidnappers, she knew what she must do.

Mulling over possibilities, she realized that to look out for the other two children, she would be forced to recruit outside help, probably from the marshal's office.

When Dylan had first told her about how the trade was to take place she had been astounded. In the movies, criminals always chose an out-of-the-way site. These men had told Dylan to meet them at a fancy shopping mall in the Uptown District of Houston. The development consisted of the Galleria for shopping, an office complex, two luxury hotels and a private health club. Actually, it was a perfect place for a person to blend into a crowd and escape, if necessary.

Palming her cell phone, Grace shooed the children into the rear yard to play while she carried out her strategy. Clouds were beginning to scud across the formerly clear sky and the wind had picked up enough that she could predict a storm in the near future. Ironically, the weather matched the dark, frightening turbulence in her heart and mind.

It was Marshal Serena Summers who picked up the phone this time. "Summers."

"This is Mary Grace Appleby," she began, cupping the tiny phone in her hands and turning her back to the house and the gusty wind so her thick, red hair would fully mask what she was doing.

"Has there been more trouble? Your husband called about a half hour ago and told us to stand down because you'd located Kyle."

"We...we know where he is. Sort of. It's a lot more complicated than what Dylan told you."

"McCall is in the car with me. I'm going to put you on speaker so he can listen, too. Okay?"

"Fine. I'm probably going to need help from both of you."

Launching into as complete an explanation as she could, Grace filled the marshals in on everything that had happened since Marshal Phillips had been called away. She concluded with, "Do you know where the Galleria is?"

"The mall near your neighborhood?"

"Yes. That's where Dylan is going to try to trade himself for Kyle. I don't trust these people to keep their word under any circumstances. I can't understand how he can."

"He may not," Summers said flatly. "What he's doing is exactly the kind of thing we always warn against."

Grace had to strain to hear what the woman was saying over the background noise of the car in which the marshals were traveling and the increasingly inclement weather on her end of the line. "I know. But he won't listen to me. He thinks there's a leak in your office and worries that would jeopardize Kyle if the information filtered back to the men he's preparing to meet."

"I can see his point," McCall replied soberly. "We both can. How much time do we have before Dylan makes his move?"

"It's set for seven, tonight, in front of the men's clothing and tuxedo rental shop on the second level of the mall. He's supposed to show up, then hang around and wait for further directions. I'd assumed the exchange would take place right there, but now that I've listened to myself telling you about it, I'm not so sure. What if they give him a message to go somewhere else after you've set a trap in the mall? How will you follow him?"

The mumbling on the other end of the line frustrated Grace. Finally she ran out of patience and raised her voice. "Well?"

"Does your husband have more than one pair of shoes, Mrs. Appleby?"

"He has a pair of cowboy boots that he wears most of the time. Why?"

"Because there's something you need to do for us," McCall told her. "Inside the luggage we issued to you there's a tiny transmitter. Run your hand around the inside seams of the side pocket. When you feel something smaller than a pea and almost totally flat, that will be the tracking device. Pull it loose and hide it in the boots, then make sure he wears them tonight. Understand?"

"Perfectly." She hesitated, deciding to be totally open and aboveboard with the pair of agents. "I plan to be there, too. We don't have a car anymore so Dylan will have to take a cab. I've arranged to leave the house ten minutes after he does."

Hearing muttering, she added, "Don't bother telling me I'm making a mistake or being careless. I've thought this through, believe me. I know the police are short-handed because of the search for Kyle and whoever took him not only knows where we live, they'll know Dylan will be gone tonight. If the other kids and I stay here we'll be worse sitting ducks than if we go to the mall and mingle with the shoppers."

"You do have a valid point," the female marshal conceded. "However, it would be better if we sent one of our people to stay with you until this is all over."

"By *over,* I assume you mean when Dylan either succeeds or fails to get our boy back, not until after the trial for child-stealing."

"Yes, ma'am. We're already making arrangements to move you again, farther away this time."

"Where to?"

"Sorry. We can't say yet."

Sighing, Grace understood completely. "The hoodlum who called said that two of my children are responsible for outing us. Is that true?"

"It looks likely," Josh McCall replied. "Listen. Stay put till one of us gets there. We should arrive in plenty of time to set up a sting operation and contact you again with specific instructions. Whatever you do, don't follow your husband to the mall tonight."

"That's exactly what I'd planned to do."

"I'd figured as much." Grace could tell how frustrated he was becoming even before he said, "Look, Grace, we're pretty short-handed. If we miss you at home, one of us will meet you at the mall tonight and take you and the kids into protective custody there."

"Okay." Grace cast a brief, sidelong glance at the house when she heard the door bang. "I have to go. Dylan's coming. I'll go fix his boots right now."

She ended the call before anyone had a chance to say goodbye and slipped the phone into her pocket.

"Everything okay out here?" Dylan asked, joining her.

"Fine. Would you mind watching these two while I run into the house for a minute?"

"Okay," Dylan said with a soft smile. "Hurry back. I'll miss you."

"Not half as much as I'll miss you if anything happens to you tonight."

"Don't go borrowing trouble," he warned. "You know you're supposed to 'Trust in the Lord with all your heart and lean not unto your own understanding.'"

"Easy to quote and very hard to do," Grace countered, stifling a shiver. "Particularly since some lowlife took my son."

It was difficult for Dylan to concentrate on anything besides his upcoming meeting with the men who had snatched Kyle. He was going through the motions of a seminormal day with his family but it was all an act, both for their benefit and for his. If he allowed himself to think too deeply he started to become overly emotional. That was unacceptable. It was bad enough that Grace kept sniffling and blowing her nose.

It was also dangerous to let his feelings take charge. The more he did that, the less chance he had of coming out of this challenge in one piece. Kyle had to be foremost in his mind and heart. Moreover, he had to concentrate on his faith; on trusting God no matter what. As long as the slightest doubt remained, it meant he was relying on himself too much.

He saw her returning with four bottles of cool water and almost managed a genuine smile.

"I decided I was thirsty," she said, handing two of the plastic bottles to him. "Hold mine while I give these to the kids?"

"Sure."

Dylan could not have torn his gaze from her if he'd wanted to. Every glance into those sky-blue eyes made his pulse jump. Every glint of light from her burnished red hair tugged at his heart until he thought he'd burst with pride and appreciation. And fear. Always the lurking fear.

He placed the water in the dappled shade at the edge of the wooden back porch and sat next to it. With his elbows resting on his knees, his hands clasped between them, he began to twist his wedding band and think back to the day Gracie had placed it on his finger.

They had been so young back then, so eager for a life together, that failure was inconceivable. As the children came along, their chances to spend quiet time appreciating each other had dwindled, of course, yet they had still shared their hopes and dreams until... *Until when?* he asked himself, realizing he had no idea what to answer.

There had been no big arguments, no pivotal point at which they had decided to call it quits and separate; it had simply happened. Truth to tell, they had drifted so far apart he hadn't been particularly surprised to be served with divorce papers. And then the rest of his world had come crashing down when he'd been picked up in connection with the baby-stealing racket.

Dylan heaved a sigh. In a twisted way, it was that crisis that had caused him to step back and reevaluate his entire life. Not only had he made poor choices for even worse reasons, he had turned his back on the things he should have valued most: his family and his faith.

Grace. Watching her toss her head and interact with the children as the wind fluttered her beautiful hair, Dylan realized this might be his last opportunity to open his heart and make her believe how penitent he was. To explain how he had done his best to turn his life around and be the kind of husband she could respect. They couldn't go back. He knew that. But he desperately wanted her to know how much he loved her before...

He could not bring himself to admit that his plan was flawed, that it might cost him dearly. Where there was life, there was hope, right? And where there was faith? Dylan slowly shook his head. It was his belief in God, his commitment to Jesus Christ, that kept reminding him of the possibility he could soon go to heaven.

Not that he was anywhere near ready to leave this earth, he insisted, he was merely aware that anything could happen. He had prayed fervently for divine aid and believed it would come. The uncertainty lay in not knowing what form God's assistance might take.

Filled with conflicting emotions, he got to his feet as his wife left the children and came toward him. If he could have sent a wish list straight to Glory he would have done so, but he knew prayer didn't work that way. As a Christian, it was his job to turn his cares over to the Lord and leave them there. Ultimately, he knew he could do that. It was what took place in the interim, what temporal choices he made, that were up to him.

So that had to be his prayer, Dylan realized, focusing his thoughts as Grace closed the distance between them.

Lord, help me do the right thing, the best thing for the loved ones you've given me.

She hesitated only slightly before stepping into his open arms.

Searching for tender words and finding none at the ready, he closed his eyes and did the only thing he could. He kissed his teary-eyed wife and thanked God for this time together.

Grace wondered why the marshals had not contacted her again if they were going to be delayed. When hours passed and she had heard nothing from them she began to get even more antsy. Naturally, Dylan noticed.

"Settle down, honey. You're going to wear yourself out," he said.

"I can't help it. I just keep thinking about Kyle and…" Once again her voice faltered and tears threatened.

"I know. But we need to stay calm for the sake of the other kids."

"They're in the back bedroom watching cartoons on a DVD because I don't want to scare them, but it was all I could do to let them out of my sight." She fought hard for self-control as she eyed him from head to toe. "I laid out clean clothes for you."

"Why? I didn't plan to change."

Her breath caught. He wasn't wearing his boots! "I think you look handsome in your jeans and Western stuff. Why not wear that?"

"It never occurred to me."

"Please?" Short of begging she had no idea how to influence the stubborn man to put on the boots with the tracking device inside. She'd thought about wedging it under the insole but had discovered plenty of room in the pointy toe so that's where she'd stuck it. Once it was in place she'd inverted the boot and given it a shake to make sure the bug stayed put. Satisfied, she'd decided to lay out a complete change of clothes in the hope that would motivate Dylan.

He got to his feet and stretched. "Okay, I'll humor you, although I can't see any reason to get all dressed up to meet a bunch of criminals. I'm sure they'll be impressed enough when I show up at all."

His glib attitude made Grace angry. "Hey, if you're going to do something this stupid you may as well look your best."

In the back of her mind she started to envision his photo in the news with captions like Local Man Gunned Down in Fashion Mall or Lawyer Shot Foiling Kidnapping. And they kept popping back into her mind as if they were little toy rubber balls on elastic thread and her brain was a wooden paddle to bounce them off.

For all the good my mind is doing me right now, it might as well be a piece of dead wood, she told herself in disgust. This was the time for keen wits, not confusion and cluttered thoughts.

Grace sighed and shook her head, staring at the doorway Dylan had passed through. There had been a time, many years ago, when she had not only chosen his suit, shirt and tie combinations, she had helped him tie a perfect knot and then straightened his collar so it lay flat.

When had she stopped doing that? And why? Perhaps it was because Dylan had started keeping such long hours, returning home late and leaving so early that she was barely awake. His job had meant the world to him. How sad that he was no longer going to be able to practice law.

Her wan smile appeared naturally as he returned, as fully Western as a cowboy who had just ridden a bucking bronco at a rodeo.

"Well?" he asked.

"Fine," Grace said, unable to counteract the somber mood that hung in the air like icy mist on a winter's morning.

As she watched, Dylan rechecked his silent cell phone and slipped it into the pocket of his jeans. Outside, a horn honked.

"That'll be my cab," he said, starting for the front door.

"Wait!" The emotional outburst slipped past her waning self-control before she could squelch it.

Dylan stopped, his hand on the knob, and turned a quizzical expression toward her.

"I—I want to say goodbye."

She closed the distance between them and reached to cup his cheeks before standing on tiptoe and giving him a heartfelt kiss.

Over the years she and Dylan had shared many kisses, some better than others, but there had never, ever, been one that had transmitted this much sentiment. This much tenderness. This much restrained passion. He set her away. "I have to go."

"Bring him home to me. Promise."

"I will."

What she yearned to hear was his solemn vow that he would come back to her, too. But she could not demand that. Their son was depending upon his father to rescue him, God willing. The Lord had to be looking out for Kyle, she argued. The boy was just an innocent bystander. All he had done was lose his temper the way any child would when faced with catastrophic events over which he had no control.

It occurred to Grace that she had done the same thing. And, even knowing it was unsuitable, she was still so mad at Dylan and so conflicted about her true feelings for him she could barely think straight.

Dylan had thought he was helping orphans when he was actually breaking the law on behalf of a bunch of low-life crooks. Yes, he'd been wrong, but could she continue to fault him when she knew he'd thought he was doing the right thing? Making the best choices? At least that was what she now believed.

With a heavy heart and an ache that filled her soul she watched her husband walk toward the waiting taxi. Rain was beginning to fall, as expected.

Then, she turned away and confirmed her order for a second cab. This was it. The most important event of her life, of her family's future, was about to take place. Was she ready?

The queasiness in the pit of her stomach and the taste of bile on her tongue told her otherwise.

Intestinal fortitude—and faith—carried her forward just the same. If this was to be the hour when she saw her husband suffer to give her back her son, she would face the event with courage and rely upon the Lord.

Without her faith to fall back on she knew she would have curled up in a fetal position and given in to the fear of a mother for her son. Fear that was showing no mercy and clawing at her heart like a snarling, hungry tiger.

NINETEEN

Traffic had moved slower than Dylan had expected, no doubt due to the increasing severity of the storm.

"Where to now?" the taxi driver asked when they reached the Galleria parking lot.

"Get as close to a main door as you can so I don't get soaked," he replied. "That one over there looks good."

"Gotcha. You been watchin' the weather radar? This is gonna be a real ripper."

"Terrific. Just what I need," he grumbled, shoving a twenty at the man and telling him to keep the change.

It was already six forty-five. He went straight to the site map kiosk to plot his course, then raced up an interior stairway rather than take the elevator or walk to an escalator that was even farther away.

From the railing skirting the second-floor walkway he could look down on the indoor skating rink. Above, the glass atrium had darkened and was beginning to be pelted by what looked and sounded like hail.

He took up a position in front of the store he'd been told to seek out and checked his cell again for the time. It had taken him fewer than five minutes after leaving the cab to reach his goal.

Now, all he could do was wait. And pray. There were no words that were adequate; no pleas as desperate as those that were unspoken and rose directly from his pounding heart to his heavenly Father.

Dylan didn't try to speak his prayers. He merely closed his eyes and let his wounded, burdened spirit do it for him.

Grace could stand it no longer. She called the marshal's cell number. "Where are you?"

"Setting up at the mall," Marshal Summers said. "Your guards have been delayed. Just stay put at the house and wait for them till we tell you otherwise."

"No way. I'm not going to let Kyle down." She had trouble swallowing past the cottony feel of her throat. "Tell me where to meet you and I'll bring the kids."

"All right. Main entrance. There's a covered area right outside the doors. We'll have someone waiting there."

"Gotcha. On my way."

She folded her youngest inside her jacket to shield him and slipped a makeshift raincoat over Beth. She'd cut holes in a black plastic trash bag, then pulled it over the girl's head. It wasn't fashionable but it did the trick.

Ignoring her daughter's wails of protest over being dressed like a walking sack of trash, Grace hurried toward the honking taxi and fastened both children in the rear seat with the help of the driver. She and he were both dripping by the time they climbed into the front.

"The Galleria," Grace said, pushing at her bangs and flipping her head to get wet hair out of her eyes. "As fast as you can."

He chuckled and used a bandanna to dry his own face before putting the car in gear. "No speeding in this kind of weather, lady. Sorry. I'm real fond of living." He patted the cab's dash. "And so is my baby here."

"Fine. Just do your best. Do you happen to know roughly where the men's tuxedo rental store is?"

"Hmm. I think it's upstairs."

"I know that. But it's a gigantic mall."

"I can drop you by a big-name department store. I'm sure it's near one of those. My wife usually starts on the ground floor and then rides the store elevator so she can shop for towels and stuff before she checks out the little shops on the second level."

"Fine. But I have to get out at the main entrance. I'm meeting somebody."

"Everybody should have stayed home tonight," the driver said with a chuckle. "It's rainin' cats and dogs."

Grace barely glanced at him. She was peering out at traffic and counting the side streets, trying to determine how close they were to their destination, since falling water obscured the street signs.

"Know where that saying came from?" he asked pleasantly, looking over his shoulder at the children. "Guess."

Beth was pouting but Brandon was willing to play. "God put dogs in the clouds?"

"Nope. Good guess though. In the olden days, when roofs were made out of bundles of straw, mice would hide in the straw and make nests. Dogs and cats went up there to chase them, and when it rained hard like this and the straw got slippery, they sometimes fell through." He guffawed. "Can you imagine? Raining cats and dogs. Right into the house!"

"Wow." Brandon was awed though not convinced. "Is that so, Mama?"

"What? Oh, yes. I think so."

"*I* want a roof with dogs and cats in it," the toddler said.

At that moment Grace would have settled for any kind of protection from the deluge, with or without animals. She dreaded having to get the kids out of the cab and make a run for the mall. Beth would stay relatively dry but she and Brandon were bound to be drenched.

The driver turned and entered the first Galleria driveway they came to. Grace was so anxious by that time she had to stop herself from pounding on the dash with her fists and yelling for him to go faster. She clenched her hands so tightly that her nails bit into her palms.

"Please hurry."

"There's a slow speed limit in here, lady. I have to keep the rules."

Rules, Grace thought, chagrined. *Always more rules.* And seemingly positioned to cause her difficulty, as usual, she added.

She'd stuffed a few necessities into her pockets rather than tote a purse and had set her phone on vibrate. Pulling out some folding money, she checked the cell phone in case the movement of the taxi had kept her from noticing. No one had called. Not even the marshals, meaning their plans to meet her at the entrance were still on. "Here we are, nice and dry," the driver told her, smiling. "Want help getting the kids out?"

"No. I can do it. Thanks."

They'd stopped under a portico and Grace was disappointed that she couldn't spot whoever was supposed to meet her.

Paying the driver and grabbing her children by the hands, she waited for the automatic door to sense her, then rushed through the gap before it was finished opening. There were plenty of shoppers on hand but none looked the least bit like a marshal or a local cop. *Now* what? She couldn't hand her children over to a stranger, so she'd have to keep them with her, at least for the present. Logic said she'd encounter the authorities soon. There was no time to waste if she hoped to be on hand when Kyle was released.

Brandon's feet were barely touching the floor on each third or fourth stride and Beth wasn't even trying to keep pace so Grace ended up practically dragging both of them.

Ahead lay an up escalator. She almost collided with an

aisle display of fragrant lotions as she zigzagged her way toward it. Beth was whimpering. Giggling, Brandon seemed delighted to be on such an exciting adventure.

"Fingers off the rail so they don't get pinched," Grace announced, stepping onto the bottom step as it rose. Beth landed on the second one back while Brandon was hoisted up next to Grace. "Beth. Keep up."

The girl began to sniffle instead. Grace was able to reason well enough, despite her current frenzy, to guess what Beth's problem was. And the child was right. They should do all they could to keep from attracting undue attention. Reaching back, she grabbed the pointed top of the black plastic bag, jerked it free and crumpled it up. "There. Better?"

The red curls bobbed an emphatic *yes*.

"Good. Now keep close to me. I mean it. This is very important. And if either of you spot your daddy, I don't want to hear a peep out of you. Understand?"

"Where's Daddy?" the little boy asked.

"I don't know yet. We're going to try to find him but it's a game, like hide-and-seek. If we see him we have to hide and wait for him to find us. We can't run up to him and make a lot of noise or it will spoil everything."

Although both children nodded, Grace was far from reassured. She was not only going to have to find Dylan without him seeing her, she was going to have to try to keep the kids from blowing her cover until she could turn them over to the marshals for safekeeping, as planned.

If they had set a trap for the criminals, she didn't want to inadvertently put her family or any bystanders in harm's way.

Stepping off the escalator and making sure her children were in the clear, Grace momentarily scanned the landing for possible threats as well as allies. One of her biggest problems was deciding who were the bad guys, who might be undercover cops and which were regular shoppers. Half the folks she saw right now looked sinister and nobody looked a bit like a U.S. marshal or a police officer.

That was not good. Not good at all.

Dylan couldn't stand still one more second. He strolled slowly to the stainless-steel railing that bordered the second-floor walkway and looked down. The mall wasn't nearly as crowded as he'd expected it to be, probably due to the nasty storm.

Since he didn't know how far Kyle's kidnappers were going to have to come to join him, he insisted it wasn't a bad sign if they were a little late. He would wait. No matter how long it took.

He was about to return to the storefront when he thought he glimpsed a flash of familiar hair color. Kyle? The sight was so fleeting he wondered if his brain was playing tricks on him. It was entirely possible that, because he so wanted to be with his son, he was imagining seeing him. That had to be what had happened. The red color was no longer visible no matter how hard he stared into the distance.

One step away from the rail, then two. On the third he felt a presence at his elbow and heard a man's deep voice say, "Just keep walking."

"Wait! Where's my son? Where's Kyle?"

"I'm taking you to him."

"I thought we were going to make the trade here."

"That was the plan until the weather turned. The boss figured we'd have trouble getting away on account of all this rain, so you and me 're gonna take a little ride."

"Okay."

If Dylan had had law-enforcement backup waiting to capture the kidnappers he would have worried about leaving the mall. In this case, it didn't matter. The way he had things figured, he'd be fortunate to live long enough to see

Kyle released. After all, if these men wanted to insure his silence, there was no better way than to kill him quickly. He only hoped the deposition he'd recorded for the marshals would be enough to get a conviction and break up the baby-stealing ring.

Instead of leading him to the escalator or elevator, as he'd expected, the thug shoved him through a door marked Maintenance. No Admittance.

The bang of the door slamming echoed along a deserted back stairway that led to the main floor. Instead of reentering the public area of the mall, however, they continued to descend.

A black SUV was waiting in an underground parking garage, its motor running, when Dylan and his companion reached the end of the line.

"Let the boy go here," Dylan ordered. "Just point him to the stairs and he'll be fine."

Both his captors laughed. The driver snorted while the other man forced Dylan into the vehicle at gunpoint.

To his horror and despair, they were the only ones present. There was no sign of Kyle.

Grace gave thanks when she spotted her husband. She took her eyes off him for mere moments. When she looked back, he was gone!

Scooping up Brandon so she could move faster, she ordered Beth, "Keep up with me," and increased her pace. If she got too close she might ruin Dylan's plans but she had to be near enough to see what was happening. *And to take charge of Kyle,* she added, feeling her pulse jump even higher than it already was.

She stepped into the doorway of a home décor shop, then eased out just enough to scan the walkway ahead. No Dylan. *And no marshals, either.*

Dismayed, she took the time to evaluate each person

she could see from there. Several looked familiar. When Serena Summers turned around and spoke into her cell phone, Grace gasped. They were here, after all. So what had become of Dylan?

One more look satisfied Grace. She stepped into view and started to approach Summers, noting that Josh Mc-Call was with her.

Marshal McCall scowled at Grace before speaking to the man beside him. "Tell our people to call off the search in her neighborhood. We've got her." His gaze met and held Grace's. "What are you doing, Mrs. Appleby? Don't you think your husband can get into enough trouble on his own?"

"I told you people I was coming here." She stood tall, demonstrating courage and determined to prove her reasons were valid. "I didn't intend to sit home where I'd be defenseless."

Marshal Summers inclined her head to her partner. "I told you what would happen if we didn't put an agent in her house with her immediately. You just don't understand women, Josh."

"If the local cops had been on the ball they'd have pulled her cab over long before she got here." He waved at a uniformed, female officer. "Over here."

Grace figured the marshal was planning to hand her over to the police and had already decided how she was going to react. As soon as the deputy joined them she forced a smile and presented her children. "This is Beth," Grace said, placing her hand first on the girl's head, then on the boy's. "This is Brandon. I'm going to trust you with them."

"Oh, no, you don't," McCall countered loudly. "I want this officer to take all three of you to the station. You'll wait there until I tell you it's safe to leave."

"Are you going to arrest me?" Grace asked, facing him with her hands fisted on her hips. "Because if you don't,

I'm going to be right behind you while you track Dylan. You wouldn't have a clue about where he was if I hadn't helped you. You owe me."

"How do you know he's not in the tuxedo shop?"

"Because you're not trying to stay out of sight. If he hadn't left you'd still be in hiding, waiting for his contact to show up."

Serena Summers smiled. "She's got you there."

"Yeah." McCall turned aside to speak into a radio. "Parking garage? Lower level? Copy. Pick us up there."

"Our lookouts spotted Dylan being shoved into a black SUV. There was no sign of the boy." He motioned to a nearby security guard. "We'll need the fastest way to reach the basement garage."

"Follow me."

Grace could tell that the elderly guard was excited to play even a small part in such an important operation. She was deathly nervous, herself, with a roiling queasiness topped by wave after wave of despair. Any time she allowed herself to picture Dylan and Kyle facing peril, she wanted to break down and weep.

I will not cry, she insisted, biting her lip for distraction and joining the party of marshals, officers and mall security guards.

It was not hard to keep up with them. The difficulty lay in keeping her balance and convincing her knees to support her. Every nerve in her body was tingling. Every step was a supreme effort. Every breath was insufficient to the point of wanting to gasp for air.

They reached the garage in a group. McCall commandeered the first of three black sedans and climbed in with his driver and the tech who was monitoring the tracking chip in Dylan's boot.

Summers took Grace's arm. "You ride with me. What

Josh doesn't know won't hurt him and I know better than to try to ditch you."

"I won't get in your way, I promise. I just have to be there for my little boy."

"And his father?"

Nodding, Grace sighed and whispered a heartfelt, "Yes."

Summers slammed her door and gave the signal to follow the lead vehicle. You could have knocked Grace over with a feather when the marshal twisted in her seat and asked, "Do you know why I'm letting you come along?"

Grace was fumbling to fasten the seat belt. "No."

"Because you place love and loyalty above your own well-being. Just don't make me sorry I brought you."

"I won't," Grace vowed. Silently she also promised she would not stand by and watch while her family was further damaged. The situation was already so dire she feared they would never be whole again, never find the happiness that had once been within their grasp.

To make that journey, to reach completeness, Grace knew they must all arrive safely on the other side of this theoretical test of fire. Like Daniel in the lion's den, she must trust in the Lord or be consumed by evil.

That concept might sound overly dramatic to someone who had never experienced the kinds of trials she was facing, who had managed to sail through life relatively easily, but for Grace it was almost an understatement.

She could not articulate her faith as well as some believers did, yet reliance upon Christ was so much a part of her being she knew she would fail miserably without Him.

What about success? she wondered. Was that going to come in the manner she had prayed for? Or should she prepare for the worst?

Realizing that her inner peace was not dependent upon the external, she took a deep breath and tried to see the current situation from God's perspective, to imagine what solution He might choose and to ready herself to accept it.

She clasped her hands, squeezed her eyes closed and bit her lower lip, trying to blot out the agonizing mental picture of a life without her firstborn son and his father at her side.

It was impossible. Her mind refused to release the picture and move forward into the unknown.

TWENTY

The lights of downtown Houston were left behind as the SUV bearing Dylan and his captors raced into the rainy night. Sheets of water dashed against the windshield so hard and fast that the wipers could not keep up.

"You tryin' to get us killed?" the thug in the rear seat with Dylan shouted.

"No. I'm tryin' to keep the cops from catchin' us," the driver yelled back. "You wanna drive?"

By this point, Dylan had decided that the wisest thing he could do was sit tight and wait. It was evident from his captors' conversation that they were not the brains of this operation. Not even close. Therefore, he still had hope that he'd ultimately be able to free Kyle and return him to his mother.

And beyond that? He refused to plan ahead even a few moments. If he had learned anything during this trying experience, it was that life was fleeting. The Bible said a man's days were numbered and the more time he spent dealing with his current dilemma, the more certain he was that his were about to end.

Dylan gritted his teeth as the heavy car bumped along a rutted, pothole-pitted dirt track. Even with the overhanging clouds and pelting rain to distort his view, Dylan knew there was no artificial light outside the vehicle. Wherever they were taking him, it was definitely secluded and probably well hidden from prying eyes. *Or those of the police,* he added, chagrined.

The driver had been leaning over the steering wheel for several miles, peering out as if expecting to spot someone or something. Lightning flashed. He jerked, straightened and hit the brakes. "There! I see him."

"About time," the man on Dylan's left remarked. "I'll be glad to get rid of this guy. He's creepin' me out."

"How so?"

"He's too quiet, like he's makin' plans or something."

"Won't make any difference if he is. This is the end of the line."

When the man poked a gun into his ribs and laughed, it sent a shiver of dread down Dylan's spine and caused him to tense every muscle. Assuming something deadly was going to happen and hearing it actually spoken about were two very different things. It seemed inconceivable after he'd come this far, had learned so much about his own character and had rededicated his life to the Lord, that it would soon end. Where was the sense in that? Where was the divine *grace?*

That word snapped him out of his doldrums. His Gracie was the key to it all. It was for her and their children that he had put himself in so much jeopardy. And it was for them that he would take whatever punishment his captors dished out.

I don't want to leave them behind, Dylan prayed silently, unable to form the kind of perfect plea that others in church often presented. He figured he was doing well to think at all, let alone come across as lucid, when a loaded automatic was aimed at him and he was about to be thrown to the wolves, so to speak.

The headlights of the SUV outlined a dark form that was almost fully hidden by the falling rain. Dylan couldn't tell much about the car they were rendezvousing with, other than the fact it looked equal in size and shape to the one in which he was traveling.

"You guys sit tight till I make sure he wants to do it here," the driver ordered.

A shiver shot up Dylan's spine and prickled the short hairs on the nape of his neck. Were they going to just shoot him? It sure sounded like it. And if they did that, what about Kyle?

"You have to release my son," he insisted. "You promised."

"Not us," the remaining man told him while the driver slogged through the mud and rain to confer with the party in the other car. "We don't give orders, we take 'em."

Dylan huffed. "Yeah, I know the feeling. It was taking orders to expedite adoptions that got me where I am tonight."

The thug guffawed. He seemed about to speak when they both saw the headlights from the other car flash. "That's our signal. Come on. Get moving."

As Dylan exited the car he felt the pressure of the gun barrel against his back. Fear made his knees weak. Faith kept him standing and walking boldly forward.

The sight of his son, alive and well, running toward him through the downpour, lifted his heart and made any sacrifice worthwhile.

Dylan's only remaining regret was that he had failed to tell Grace how much he loved her when he'd had a chance.

Radio chatter was kept to a minimum, meaning the marshals relied heavily on their cell phones as long as they still had a signal. When they lost that, they fell back on their radios.

It did nothing to calm Grace's nerves to sense that the pros were as nervous as she was. That did not bode well for poor little Kyle. Or for her husband.

Thinking of them as a family unit, she was reminded of Solomon's wise advice about dividing a baby to see which woman was its real mother. In her case, the division was about to take place and she was likely to lose at least one of the halves; either Kyle or his father.

There was no way her finite mind could handle thoughts like that, yet when she tried again to redirect it she failed miserably. All she could think of was her loved ones and their plight. For her, there was nothing else.

The radio barked in the front seat. Marshal Summers leaned forward to listen, then said, "All right, Grace. It looks like the SUV carrying your husband has stopped. Some of us are going to get out and circle around so we can come at them from all sides. You're to stay right here."

"But I…"

Summers shook her head emphatically. "No buts. I was taking a big chance by bringing you along. If you don't follow my orders you might get hurt. Or, worse, you might cause us to have to hold our fire so the men who took your husband and the boy escape. You certainly don't want that to happen."

"Of course not."

"Then stay put and let us do our jobs. As soon as we have Kyle, someone will bring him to you."

"Promise?"

"Promise," the marshal said. "I'll do everything I can to make this work. Believe me, I know how it feels to lose someone you love."

Watching the others move away from both official cars and blend into the landscape, Grace wished she hadn't put Beth's plastic bag in the trash. If she still had it she could at least step out without getting soaked.

Her hand rested on the door handle in the backseat, her fingers itching to give it a yank. She'd noticed that the dome light had stayed off when the others climbed out so surely opening her door wouldn't attract undue attention. At least she might be able to hear more. Being stuck in the closed vehicle was akin to sitting in a soundproofed room. She couldn't bear not to know what was going on, no matter the risk to her personal safety.

Cautiously, Grace eased open the car door and slid out. Precipitation had slacked off but the electrical storm hung on, lighting the stormy sky and giving her goose bumps when thunder clapped on the heels of the original flash.

The following boom sounded so close it made her hair prickle. She ducked, pressing her body to the side of the car. "I should be inside so the rubber tires can insulate me," she told herself.

Another bolt shot to earth. Then another. Grace reached for the exterior door handle and pulled. Nothing happened! Had she inadvertently locked herself out? Or could the official car have been engineered that way to prevent theft or tampering?

She duck-walked to the opposite side. It, too, was locked. Which left as her only option the lead car that had transported Josh McCall and a few deputies.

Making it from her present position to the other car would have been simple if there had not been falling rain coupled with a rough road and almost no ambient light.

Grace waited for more lightning to show her the best course, then started off while the picture of the terrain was still glowing. "Just a little farther," she murmured, wiping her wet face with her hand and pushing long bangs off her forehead.

The next flash brought her the final few feet to the car's rear bumper. She paused, wondering if there was anyone left to guard it or if all the other agents had gone with Marshals Summers and McCall.

The next boom came without a flash. Grace instinctively ducked, realizing belatedly that this particular noise was different than what she'd been hearing. This was more like a crack, high-pitched yet resonant.

She started to straighten, to peer in the direction of the noise. It came again, this time with a flash that began and ended on her level. *That was gunfire!*

Her heart clenched. Were the marshals shooting at the kidnappers? Would they do that knowing that Dylan and Kyle were present? Perhaps they'd be forced to return fire if the crooks had shot at them.

Which meant they'd located their quarry and were closing in. She couldn't just stand there while her family was being shot to pieces. She had to help.

Before Grace could decide what to do next, a hooded figure came at her through the rain and mist. Initially she thought the man was enormous. Then she realize he was carrying something that made him seem much taller.

Rising, she showed herself in spite of the sporadic firing that continued in the distance.

The black-draped figure reached the lead car and ducked beside it.

When he straightened moments later, he had a pistol pointed directly at Grace. "What are you doing here?"

Because Dylan had not been tied or handcuffed, he was able to fend for himself when the shooting started. He had not seen Kyle, nor was he sure who the combatants were, but he assumed at least some of them were on his side. Being caught in the crossfire was bad enough without finding out that both sides were intent on doing you in.

Beyond his position he heard a man scream, then moan for a moment before falling silent.

Another bullet broke a car window above his head, sending shards of glass raining down on him. He crawled forward, searching for his son. If he'd dared take the chance on Kyle answering and giving himself away, he'd have shouted for him.

Other voices were raised. Until Dylan knew who had won the battle he was not about to reveal his position.

"Got him!" someone yelled.

"Then get him out of here," was the answer.

Could they be referring to Kyle? Had his sacrifice been enough? Dylan's breath failed him. He used the side of the car to pull himself to his feet.

That had to be it, he insisted, already praising God in his heart and mind. Kyle was safe. The marshals or other officers had rescued him!

As Dylan pivoted toward the place where he hoped to catch a glimpse of his son, more shots echoed. The first was followed by a volley but he scarcely noticed.

He was already falling.

Grace ignored the marshal and dropped to her knees to gather Kyle close, raining kisses on his wet hair and cheeks until he rebelled. "Mo-om. I'm okay. Honest."

She saw his grin through her tears and returned it as best she could. "Where's your daddy?"

The child's cocky attitude vanished. "Dad's here?"

"Yes. He arranged to trade himself for you. Didn't you see him when they let you go?"

Kyle was blinking rapidly, clearly a lot more concerned than he had been. "No. The guy who had me in his car jumped out and ran away, so I did, too." He glanced over his shoulder. "A marshal found me."

"They'd promised to bring you to me and they did." Grace gave the sopping-wet boy another squeeze and a kiss, this time without protest, then held him by the shoulders to look him straight in the eyes. Even in the near-dark she could tell he was crying.

"Your daddy is a very brave man," she said, pushing

through the emotion that kept making her voice break. "I never realized that before, at least not well enough to tell him how proud I was—I am—of him."

"You can tell him soon," Marshal Summers said from beyond the first car. "They're bringing him in."

Grace arose on quaking legs, her eldest son at her side. "They are? Is he all right? There was so much shooting I was afraid he might…"

"Oh, he's got another little nick in him but it doesn't seem to be slowing him down much."

"Dylan was shot!"

"Grazed," Summers told her. "That's a lot better than two of the three others."

"Your people are all okay?"

"Yes. And your husband would be, too, if he'd kept his head down. Which reminds me." She scowled. "What are *you* doing out of the car?"

"I just stepped out for a second and the door locked behind me. I couldn't get back in when I tried." Grace pointed. "That one's locked up tight, too."

"For your protection," Marshal McCall said as he joined them. He was assisting Dylan, although it looked to Grace as if her husband was steady enough on his own.

She left Kyle with Summers and ran to him, pausing just short of recklessly throwing herself into his arms. "Where are you hurt? I can't tell."

"Does that mean I can't have one of your special hugs until I wash this mud off?" The way he was smiling, the way his dark eyes were reflecting the glow from the headlights, told her how truly happy he was to be back with her.

That was all the encouragement Grace needed. She reached up, cupped his cheeks and pulled his face down for the first of many kisses to come. When she came up for air she whispered, "I love you, Mr. Appleby."

"I love you, too. Will you marry me?"

"I already did that once."

"I know. I just thought it might be good to start from the beginning to see if we can get it right the second time around."

"I know we can. Where shall we go on our honeymoon?"

Marshal McCall edged closer and cupped his hand around his mouth to offer, "How about Hawaii?"

"Really?" Grace was both astounded and excited. "To visit or to stay?"

"That depends on how well your kids behave themselves in this new life," McCall said flatly. "You obviously can't go home after tonight. I have hopes we'll be able to track down the one survivor and get him to talk, but there are no guarantees. He may not know who's really pulling the strings. We'll pack for you and send your belongings to our office in the islands."

Grace slipped an arm around her husband's waist, unmindful of his wet, dirty clothing. "How will Dylan testify if we're so far away?"

"He may not need to if his deposition works well. A lot will depend upon our ability to unravel the rest of the mysteries surrounding the origins of some of the babies who passed through his office."

Grace felt Dylan tensing before he said, "I've been giving that some thought. Marshal Phillips showed me a picture of one of the babies he'd helped rescue recently. I wish I could see it again."

McCall pulled out his cell phone and brought up the photo of a laughing, blond child without too much delay. "Did it look like this?"

"Yes. Is that a girl?"

"Yes. Why? Do you recognize her?"

"I didn't think so at first but while I was held prisoner I couldn't get those big blue eyes out of my mind. I think that's Isabella, Vanessa Martinez's daughter."

"What makes you think so?" Marshal Summers had joined the group and was also staring at the photo.

"Because I remember thinking how odd it was for a woman of her apparent ethnicity to have such a fair baby. She was one of the ones I thought might have been a fake after I found out about the counterfeit paperwork."

"We call her Baby C," Summers said. "Now that I have a name I should be able to trace the mother by starting with border towns."

"Try looking around El Paso first," Dylan said. "I seem to recall something about her being picked up for shoplifting before she agreed to relinquish the child. There may be a connection. I wouldn't put it past these guys to use blackmail."

Grace cuddled closer to her husband, giving thanks that his upstanding character had not only resurfaced, it had been fire-polished in the process.

Her upturned face caught his attention. "I love you, Gracie. Did I mention that?"

"Yes, but I'll never get tired of hearing you say it. I love you, too. More than ever."

"We're not the same people we were the first time we walked down the aisle," Dylan said softly, just for her.

"I know." A shining smile lit her face and her eyes twinkled as she turned her gaze toward the clearing sky and whispered, "Thank You, God."

EPILOGUE

The black sand beach was warm beneath Grace's bare feet as she stood under an arbor with her groom. He was wearing a blue-and-yellow-flowered shirt and her flattering sarong complemented it perfectly.

Beth stood beside the bride, holding her orchid bouquet while Brandon was the ring bearer and Kyle the best man. This time, Grace was mature enough to actually hear every word the preacher spoke and remember with gratitude how they had ended up there.

They were renewing their vows as Mr. and Mrs. London, Roger and Edie, while the children had been encouraged to choose their own new names. Kyle had had everyone in stitches by picking every superhero on record, finally agreeing to Clark. Beth had insisted that Elizabeth entitled her to go by Liz, and Brandon had chosen Teddy in honor of his favorite stuffed bear, one of the gigantic ones his daddy had brought home from work as a memento.

When they turned to leave the arbor, Dylan spotted a solitary figure in a dark suit standing at the edge of the lava flow that bordered one end of the beach. He nudged Gracie. "Look, Edie. We have a wedding guest."

Her first reaction was fear, followed quickly by relief when the figure waved and started toward them.

The men shook hands. Grace kept hold of her husband's

arm, unwilling to share him with Marshal McCall for even a few minutes.

"Don't look so worried," the marshal said. "I just came to check on you and to bring you some good news."

"You'll have trouble topping what just happened right here," Grace said.

"Undoubtedly. However, I thought you'd like to know that we found the Martinez woman and flew her to Missouri to be reunited with her baby. The foster parents had hoped to eventually adopt and were crushed, but at least Vanessa knows what's become of her baby. It's a good start."

"What about the guy you were looking for after the shootout in Houston? Did you find him and get him to talk?"

Grace tightened her hold on Dylan's arm when the marshal shook his head and sobered. Before he actually said so, she sensed what had happened. Another possible witness had been killed before he could be convinced to inform on his bosses.

Standing there in the warm sunshine of such a lush paradise, it was hard to imagine so many evil people and so much loss.

Given their past, she knew she and Dylan might never be totally free of worry, yet she also knew better than to complain about the blessings God had bestowed; not because they were such worthy humans, but because He was so merciful.

From now on, she vowed she would see life as the special gift it was and give thanks for every single second of it, particularly when she was sharing it with the wonderful man she had just married. *Again.*

* * * * *

Dear Reader,

This was a very special book for me. It helped lead me to a much deeper faith. As God led me to see the fragility of life through Grace McIntyre's eyes, He helped me heal in my personal life. Because the Lord had prepared me, I made it through. And I'm stronger for it. I pray that you will call upon Jesus in times of trouble and learn, as I did, that He is always with you.

Blessings,

Valerie Hansen

Questions for Discussion

1. Have you ever known anyone who is certain, as Dylan was, that it's okay to bend the law for a higher purpose? Is that wise?

2. How do you think the coerced mothers of the babies felt? Is it possible that some of them were okay because they felt their children would be better off?

3. I have friends who adopted wonderful kids. Is that something you might want to do or would you have trouble accepting a child that you did not actually give birth to?

4. Just because a woman gives birth, does she automatically feel a bond with her baby? If not, why might she have trouble?

5. Grace chooses the well-being of her children over her own wants and needs. Is that how a parent is supposed to feel? What might alter that choice?

6. Grace and Dylan had drifted apart slowly. Do you think Grace was right in filing for divorce? Might she have hoped that her action would wake up her husband to his faults? Is that smart?

7. Even after Dylan learns that he has been an unwitting party to crime, he still tries to justify his actions. Isn't that typical human behavior?

8. The Witness Protection Program is not foolproof. Can you imagine what it would be like to have to walk away

from everything? What's worse, the loss of family and friends or giving up earthly possessions?

9. If you had to go into witness protection, who would you miss most? Have you told them you love them? Lately?

10. The ultimate goodbye is through death. Given that possibility, would you start to see people with more empathy, the way Grace and Dylan saw each other? Can you understand why problems that had once seemed insurmountable became of little consequence in the face of mortal danger?